Together Again

Peggy Bird

CRIMSON
ROMANCE
F+W Media, Inc.

This edition published by
Crimson Romance
an imprint of F+W Media, Inc.
10151 Carver Road, Suite 200
Blue Ash, Ohio 45242

www.crimsonromance.com

ISBN 10: 1-4405-5584-2
ISBN 13: 978-1-4405-5584-8
eISBN 10: 1-4405-5585-0
eISBN 13: 978-1-4405-5585-5

Dedication

This book is dedicated, first, to the women throughout my life who have mentored, inspired and befriended me. If I haven't said it in person, let me do it now: thank you. I have no idea how I would have survived this long without my women friends.

Second, to three very special women: Rebecca, Meg and Elizabeth. You amaze me on a regular basis with what you do and who you are.

Third, to Philadelphia, a sometimes gracious lady where I spent some pretty good years.

Chapter 1

Instead of the peace and coffee she'd been looking for before boarding her plane, Margo Keyes's latte came with a side order of idiot-on-a-cell-phone. Anyone within twenty feet of the man in the blue blazer heard some of the conversation. Where she was sitting, it was in Dolby digital surround sound.

It figured her trip would start like this. She'd been apprehensive about it from the get-go. Not that she had a fear of flying. It was the landing—or rather, what was waiting for her *after* she landed—that was the problem.

Her chance for quiet acquisition of caffeine courage diminishing by the second, she glared at the man in the blue blazer, hoping he'd take the hint and shut up. Too intent on his call, he seemed to miss what was, she was quite sure, a stunning look of disapproval.

"Are you interested or not?" he yelled. Allowing no answer to what was apparently a rhetorical question, he continued, "If you don't want what I've got, I know someone who does. So, what's it worth to you?" After he paused, presumably for the response, he said, "Good. I'll let you know what the bid is after I talk to my other customer." He ended the call, shoved his phone in his pocket and glared back at Margo before storming off.

Walking down the concourse, she consoled herself that if the coffee break hadn't worked, at least she had a business class seat reserved on the plane and a hotel suite waiting at her destination. She'd indulged in both, rationalizing if she was making this trip at least it should be comfortable. Interesting concept, that: comfortable discomfort.

As the plane taxied out to the runway, she pulled out her BlackBerry to review her schedule for the next ten days, hoping some magic wand had been waved over it, making it all shiny and fun. However, as usual, her fairy godmother was AWOL. She put her head back against the seat and closed her eyes. What the hell had she been thinking, saying yes to this? Ever since she'd moved to Portland, she'd restricted her Philadelphia visits with her mother to long weekends in the spring and fall. It got her points for being a good daughter, avoided too much time being fussed over and kept her out of the two East Coast seasons she didn't like. This trip? Ten days in mid-June when she'd just been there two months before.

Checking the airline schedule online, she found a flight home the day after the presentation she was to give the following week. That would cut three days off the trip. But before she could change her reservation, the flight attendant asked her to turn her phone off.

Nothing left to do but work. She opened her stuffed-to-the-gunnels messenger bag and took out what she'd brought to help her craft her speech. It looked like she'd included everything in the courthouse except the old law library. Being tapped as the last-minute stand-in for your boss at an important conference will make you do that.

While trying to organize it all, she lost track of her jacket. She eventually saw it too far under her seat to grab and asked the person sitting behind her to get it for her. A man threw it back. When she turned to thank him he added a dirty look—a familiar dirty look. Shit. The man in the blue blazer from the coffee stand.

Finally settled, she began to review case files. Unfortunately, the steady stream of orders to the flight attendants from the seat behind her distracted both her and the cabin crew. When she'd read the same report three times and still didn't know what the hell it was about, she gave up trying, put her work away and replaced it with her iPod. By plugging in the ear buds she could drown out ABB ("Asshole in Blue Blazer," as he had now morphed into being) with Pink Martini, Colbie Caillat, Suzanne Vega and Alicia Keys.

By the time she'd worked through most of her current favorite albums, the pilot announced their imminent arrival in Philadelphia. Winding the cord for the ear buds around the iPod before stashing it away, the thought occurred that ABB had now wrecked a second part of her day. Two strikes against her and she hadn't even gotten to the hard part yet.

The man jumped up as soon as the plane's wheels hit the ground, arguing with the flight attendant when she insisted he get back in his seat. He sprang into action again as soon as they arrived at the gate, rooting around in the compartment above Margo like he was hunting for truffles. Fearful he'd dump out the contents of her messenger bag she stood, too, and removed it from the overhead.

"Out of the way," ABB said. "I'm in a hurry."

"We all are," Margo said. "But they haven't opened the door yet."

"I have to be out of here when they do. Move, bitch."

"Excuse me? What did you . . . ?"

The man grabbed his briefcase and pin-balled his way through passengers and cabin crew to the door, which was still closed. "Asshole in Blue Blazer" moved ahead of "walking across the country pushing heavy beverage carts" on the list of reasons she was glad she hadn't followed up on that girlhood fantasy of being a flight attendant so she could get paid for traveling.

At baggage claim, still thinking of comebacks for ABB, some of which were anatomically impossible, most of which were too obscene to say out loud and many of which were both, she let her bag go past a couple times before she realized it had made an appearance. Off balance when she snagged it, she swung around awkwardly, smacking into someone behind her. When she started to apologize she saw, much to her consternation, she'd whacked— guess who?—talking again on the phone.

Echoing her sentiments, ABB said, "Oh, hell, you again. Just what I need," and elbowed past her. He grabbed the briefcase leaning up against the luggage belt in front of her, and ran toward the taxi stand, leaving her apologizing to empty air. "Welcome to Philadelphia, Margo," she muttered to no one in particular as she pulled out the handle from her suitcase.

At the exit for the rental car shuttles, she hesitated long enough to inhale one last little bit of cool, clean air. Thus prepared, she forced herself out the automatic door into the wall of hot, wet vapor, which, laced with vehicle exhaust and the effluvium of the nearby oil refineries and storage facilities, was what passed for air during summer in her birthplace.

Oh, yeah, welcome to Philly.

*

A short, stocky man in a business suit paced on the spongy ground, wiped his forehead with a handkerchief and swatted away a bug. He hated this weather. When he delivered what he was about to get, he'd be on the next plane out of here.

A taxi approached and he stepped back into the shadow of the trees. The car's interior light illuminated a man in a dark blue blazer paying the driver. After the cab peeled off, the stocky man emerged from the shadows and beckoned.

The two men walked silently into the copse of trees. When they were hidden from the road, the stocky man asked for what he'd contracted to purchase. The man in the blue blazer said he had another offer that the buyer had to meet or the deal was off. The stocky man shook his head. The man in the blue blazer pulled out his cell phone and punched in a number. He handed the phone over after the call was answered. The stocky man said a few words in a foreign language before handing the phone back to its owner.

While Blue Blazer was focused on winding up the phone

conversation, the stocky man reached under his jacket and pulled out a gun. His problem eliminated, the gunman pulled the blazer-clad body further into the trees and covered it with branches.

Taking the phone and the briefcase, he returned to his car. When he searched the briefcase, he discovered that what he wanted wasn't there. Nor, he found out when he went back and searched the body, was it in the fucking blue blazer. All he had was a flash drive with what he'd already seen and a pissed-off buyer waiting for what he now couldn't deliver.

*

In her rental car and headed toward Center City on I-95, Margo went over, again, what she had ahead of her. The shoes she'd packed said it all—Manolo Blahniks for a high school reunion she'd been conned into attending, mid-heel pumps for the conference where she was to give the still-unwritten presentation and the flats she wore to please her mother who hated running shoes. No shoes were needed for the other thing niggling at the back of her mind.

In Portland, where she was a thirty-something deputy district attorney, Margo's colleagues thought it was great she was going for a longer-than-usual visit with her mother. She'd explained her reluctance was because she didn't like the summer weather. But it wasn't just the weather she didn't want to face. There was the world of Daisy Keyes to deal with.

"Daisy" was what her maternal grandmother, for whom she was named, had called her. It was the literal translation of Margherita, her given first name. Margo was grateful no one else had joined her *abuelita* in that folly. What the hell had she been thinking? Daisy? Really?

What made it worse was she thought of herself as a wilted daisy that last year of high school, at the mercy of people and events over which she had no control. Now Margo would be spending an evening with people she largely avoided when she visited her mother, all of whom she was sure remembered only too clearly what had happened that year.

But a suite at the Bellevue would help. No memories there. And, she noticed as she looked around the lobby while waiting to register, no guy in a blue blazer either. She crossed her fingers that she'd seen the last of him. All she had to do was unpack and freshen up and she'd be ready to face whatever was waiting on Fir Street.

*

Margo and her mother, Dolores Campbell Keyes, had grown up in the same house in South Philadelphia. The three-story row house with a marble stoop and a deep-set entry had been her mother's dowry when she married Kenny Keyes. Nothing about it had changed since her grandmother had lived there, except the rest of the neighborhood.

After circling the block for only five minutes, Margo found a semi-legal parking spot, made sure nothing valuable was visible and locked up the car. As she approached her mom's house, a man called from the direction of the darkened entry immediately adjacent to it, startling her.

"Welcome home, counselor," he said.

"Tony?" She stopped, her eyes searching the row of houses. "Is that you?"

Tony Alessandro—Anthony Salvatore Alessandro to the DMV, Detective Alessandro to his employer, the Philadelphia Police Department—stepped out of the shadowy entry of the house next to the Keyes' residence. The boy-next-door for all of Margo's childhood, Tony had grown up into one of the best looking men she'd ever known—classically handsome features that would be at home in a Roman temple; hair so dark it was almost black; brown eyes that could make her knees buckle with one look. A mouth that made kissing a sacrament.

He came down the steps with the easy grace of an athlete and met her at the end of the short walkway to his mother's house. Greeting her with a hug and a lingering kiss on the cheek he said, "It's been a long time since Mary Ellen's wedding last fall."

And there it was, the last thing making her nervous about this trip. Mary Ellen's wedding. When he'd danced with her all night before sneaking her out of the parish hall to a dark Sunday school classroom where he proceeded to kiss her senseless, making her mouth burn for his, her breasts ache for him to touch them and her whole body melt into a wet and wanting puddle. If his nephew hadn't dragged him away, she was sure they'd have ended up naked in his bed. Or on the floor of the classroom.

But she hadn't heard from him since.

She knew the blush that was the bane of her existence was now creeping up her neck but hoped the dusky light concealed it. "Yeah, you weren't around when I was here in April."

"I was in DC, meeting with this task force I'm on. I hear you're back for our class reunion."

"My mother's doing, not mine. She signed me up. The half-dozen people who emailed saying how great it was I would be there made me feel guilty enough that I didn't have the nerve to back out."

"Not like you to give in to social pressure."

"Maybe I'm getting soft in my old age."

"Better work on your argument, counselor. No one who's ever met you will believe that one." He'd kept his hand on her shoulder and was studying her face. "You look great. West Coast agrees with you, doesn't it?"

"It does. As much as Philly agrees with you. Every time I see you, I wonder if there's a portrait turning wrinkled, soft and flabby in an attic somewhere. I swear to God you still look like the guy the yearbook described. Let's see: best athlete in the class with the body to show for it. A smile that would melt glaciers. Brown eyes every girl wants to get lost in." She glanced over his broad shoulders and trim body in jeans and a denim jacket, and up at his handsome face. "Yup, all still there."

He dropped his arm, laughed and made a very Italian gesture, one that even a non-Italian, at least a non-Italian from Philadelphia, would recognize. "Jesus, Margo, leave it to you to remember that shit." He motioned toward her empty hands. "Not to change the subject but, no luggage? You're not staying with your mom?"

"Impressive analytic skills. No wonder you made detective on your first try. Congratulations on that, by the way. Where're you working?"

"Thanks. I'm working with the white-collar crime unit."

She looked embarrassed. "Good choice. You had a running start on the subject fifteen years ago, didn't you?"

"Are you evading my question about where you're staying, Madame Prosecutor? Can't imagine you let witnesses do something like that."

"No, sir, Detective Alessandro, I do not. I'm staying at the Bellevue. Between a conference in Center City next week and not wanting to go to the reunion feeling like the twelve-year-old I seem to turn into when I stay here, I thought it best."

"Sounds like neither one of us is too anxious to go to this thing." He looked away from her and stuck his hands in his jeans pockets.

"Why are you worried? I thought you went to all our class reunions."

"This time, Nicole will be there."

He didn't need to say more; she knew the story. Nicole, who'd been his off-again, on-again high school girlfriend and then fiancée, broke their engagement to elope with a much older—and definitely richer—man, banging up Tony's pride badly. Neighborhood gossip said it could only have been the promise of life on the prestigious

Main Line that had won Nicole away from Tony. But then, the neighborhood always favored the Alessandro side of any story.

"I didn't think she did reunions, either."

"Not 'til this one."

"I hope you have a supermodel lined up to go with you."

"No date. You?"

"Surely the grapevine," she nodded toward their mothers' homes, "has already told you I don't." She pulled her gaze away from his and took a deep breath before blurting out, "Listen, not that I'm a supermodel, but I brought this fairly outrageous dress to wear with my new Manolo Blahniks. It might, I don't know, give our classmates something to talk about other than her if you arrive with the woman no one's seen in fifteen years, even if it is just me. And I wouldn't mind having company when I walk into that restaurant. It'd just be, you know, old friends . . ."

He held up his hand. "Slow down. So, you're volunteering to be my date?"

"I just think it might be advantageous for both of us if we went together."

"That sounds more like an offer to carpool."

"Really, just old friends doing each other a favor." She searched his face trying to anticipate his answer. "So . . . yes? No?"

"Now why would I turn down the chance to walk in with the class mystery woman in an outrageous dress and expensive shoes? Pick you up . . . when? "

"How about I pick you up? I don't think my new dress would fare well on your motorcycle."

"I'll bow to your transportation preferences. But the Bellevue's right around the corner from my apartment. I'll walk over so you won't have to look for a parking space."

"Great. Maybe come by at five and have a drink before we go so we can catch up?" The offer slipped out before she could think about it. "I'm in suite 832."

"I'll see you at five." He gave her a quick peck on the cheek. "Say hi to your mom for me."

At her mother's door, she dug around in her purse for the key, listening for the sound of Tony's cycle taking off so she could relax. Her mother opened the door before Margo could get it unlocked. "Hello, dear." She reached up and kissed her daughter. "Was that Anthony I heard?"

"Yes, Mom. He said to say hi."

Dolores Keyes' eyes lit up. "I'm glad you had a chance to talk with him. Did he say anything about the reunion? I hear he's going alone."

"He was, but we just made arrangements to go together."

"Oh, good." She pulled at her daughter's hand. "How silly to stand on the doorstep talking! I like your hair. It's a little longer than before, isn't it?" She closed the door after Margo. "Oh, and don't let me forget to give you the sticky buns I got for you."

The evening had begun the way visits with her mother always did—a comment about her hair and a bribe of sticky buns. It continued in its usual trajectory with Margo talking about Portland and her mother talking about friends and family in Philadelphia.

There was no mention of what had obsessed Margo every time she thought about this trip. But then they never discussed *that* subject.

In the fall of her senior year of high school, her father had been arrested on federal racketeering charges along with some of his clients, members of the Philly mob. All through that year, as one trial after another hit the headlines, Margo and her mother had dealt with the humiliation of learning that Kenny Keyes was not the kind of lawyer they thought he was. He'd been convicted and sent to federal prison. Dolores Keyes hadn't uttered his name since.

After they cleaned up the kitchen, Margo left, promising to join her mother and aunt the next day for lunch. But once at her hotel, she couldn't settle down. She tried convincing herself it was jet lag or maybe nervousness about seeing people she hadn't seen since high school. Eventually, she had to admit it was Tony keeping her awake.

Born a month apart to next-door neighbors, they'd been childhood playmates as well as high school classmates. His sisters were her best friends; she'd learned to dance with him when they were barely teenagers. He'd made sure she had fun down at the shore the summer after her father's trial. They hung out when she was back in Philly between college and law school. But somehow they never got beyond a close friendship, dinner-and-movie dates and some unforgettable kissing.

Maybe it was geography. They had spent most of the past fifteen years on opposite coasts, after all. Maybe they were never in the same place in their lives at the same time. Whatever it was, she'd always told herself settling for a warm, affectionate friendship was a good thing. After all, a relationship between a police officer and the daughter of a mob lawyer probably wasn't a match made in heaven.

Then his sister Mary Ellen got married.

Chapter 2

Her all-too-short night ended when the maid who wanted to make up the room knocked on the door. After a quick shower, Margo dressed and grabbed her messenger bag, heading downstairs to forage for caffeine and to make a stab at organizing her speech. A coffee cart provided her with her drug of choice; a phone call to her office should have gotten her the help she wanted. But her boss, Jeff Wyatt, wasn't around, as he usually was on Saturday mornings.

Instead she got Kiki Long, her favorite paralegal and friend, who was making a rare weekend appearance at work. No help in the speech-writing area, Kiki kept asking why Margo sounded so sleepy. Rejecting jet lag as an explanation, Kiki decided that Margo had met a man on the plane and fallen into his bed when she got to Philadelphia where she'd spent the night having the best sex of her life. As she always did when Kiki speculated on her life, Margo let her ramble. Then she left a message for Jeff.

On her own to get her presentation started, she went through her files again and made a few notes before noticing the time. Breakfast coffee had run into the lunch date she had with her mother and aunt.

Pushing through the door to Broad Street, she was greeted with both temperature and humidity already in the nineties, normal for Philly but rarely seen in Portland and never in June. Rose Festival, the city's annual celebration of all things floral, often took place in weather referred to as "June-uary." Any self-respecting Portland rosebush, not to mention the Rose Princesses' hairdos, would wilt in Philly's June weather.

The restaurant where she was meeting her mom was near City Hall, a building she'd always loved, elegantly presiding over the crossroads of Broad and Market Streets. With a statue of William Penn on top and the forty-five-foot Oldenburg clothespin across the street, it outshone Portland's more modest civic headquarters and its nearby elk statue. On the other hand, she could have done without the din of the six lanes of traffic adjacent to her path. Her adopted hometown's narrower, tree-lined streets were quieter and much more gracious.

Sometimes, though, she admitted as she strode toward her lunch date at a very un-Portland-like pace, she missed the more intense energy Philly generated. Portland's low-key, polite atmosphere sometimes made her grit her teeth. Sometimes laid-back was just a little too . . . well, laid-back.

Back in her hotel by mid-afternoon, she wondered where the day had gone. All she had to show for it was a credit card receipt for lunch and a bottle of her favorite Scotch. The nap she planned and a long soak in the tub afterwards would, she hoped, clear her head before the reunion.

After an hour's sleep, she filled the tub and turned on the jets. The bubbling was soothing and she relaxed into the warm water, her head back on a folded towel. She was on the edge of another little snooze when the phone rang—Jeff Wyatt returning her call. They discussed ideas for her speech for long enough that, when she hung up, she saw she had only a half hour before Tony arrived. She hurried to get dressed, to get the papers tidied up in the living room of the suite and to get ice cubes.

Seeing herself in a full-length mirror after donning her new dress, she wondered if what had seemed like a good idea in Portland looked a bit sluttier than she'd intended. Cobalt blue to set off her dark hair and dark blue eyes, the dress hugged her body like a second skin on the way to a hem that almost brushed her knees. One shoulder, both arms and a good part of her back were bared. All she could fit under it, other than herself, was a pair of black bikini panties.

She shrugged. Too late to back out now. It was either this, court clothes or casual pants. After slipping on the black, peep-toe Manolo Blahniks, she tamed the layered waves of her hair with a brush, dabbed on makeup, made a pass at her lashes with a mascara wand, applied lipstick, sprayed on perfume, pushed an armload of silver hoop bracelets over her hand and called it good. She was putting on some dangly earrings when there was a light rapping at the door. She glanced at the clock. Five, exactly. Tony, as always, was right on time.

And, also as always, he looked gorgeous. In place of the denim of the night before, he wore cream-colored trousers and a black linen jacket, a white shirt open at the neck, and what she was sure were Italian loafers. His short, dark hair was brushed back from his face except for the cowlick where a part might be if he had one. A curl from the cowlick punctuated his hairline with the tail of a comma. She wasn't sure if it was the curl or the spicy-sexy stuff he'd splashed on after he shaved, but something made her want to bury her hands in his hair and do things with his mouth she shouldn't be thinking about.

Realizing she needed to say something, she got out, "Oh, hi." She could feel herself begin to blush. "I mean, come on in."

He was so busy staring at her, he didn't seem to notice her stumbling over her words.

"Holy Mother of God, Margo." His voice was so low and hoarse she thought he might have picked up a cold since she'd seen him. "'Fairly outrageous' hardly does it justice."

"Too much, do you think?" she asked, smoothing the dress across her hips.

"Absolutely not. Not from where I'm standing." The kiss he gave her was definitely not perfunctory and made her wonder if he could read minds. Even more uncomfortable now, she moved away and walked to the bar.

By the time she got there, she'd regained some control. "I was just about to pour myself a drink. What would you like? I have a bottle of my favorite single malt Scotch and I have a mini-bar, your choice." She brought out two glasses, removed the lid from the ice bucket and started putting ice cubes in the glasses.

But when she turned to get his answer, she felt the floor give way and with it, her control. He was leaning on the counter, looking at her with his pools-of-chocolate eyes as if she was the only thing he wanted to see.

Now if only she could remember how to put square ice cubes into round glasses.

" . . . single malt?" His words began to come back into focus. "They must pay DAs better in Portland than they do in Philly."

"Ah . . . no. No, not really." Unsure what else he'd said, she grabbed onto the last part of his sentence. "But since I never seem to do anything except, you know, work, I splurge occasionally on good Scotch."

"I'll take advantage of your splurge, then."

She finally managed to get both the ice and the liquor into the glasses, spilling only a little. When she'd handed his to him, she led him to the living area. He settled back at one end of the sofa while she sat at the other, sipping carefully at her drink, caught again by his candy bar eyes and hesitating to mix too much Scotch with all that chocolate.

"How was your day? You spend it with your mom?" he asked.

"Some of it. We had lunch, did a little shopping. Before that, I worked on a speech I'm giving next week. Didn't get very far, but it was better than yesterday."

"What happened yesterday? Bad flight?"

"The flight was fine. It was this Asshole in a Blue Blazer. He bugged me in the airport when I was drinking my coffee. Kept up such a racket on the plane I couldn't work. Then, when I hauled my suitcase off the luggage belt, I accidently hit him with it, so he swore at me and pushed me aside to get to the taxi stand."

"Yo, welcome to Philly." He raised his glass in a mock toast.

"My thoughts exactly. But as long as he's somewhere in the Delaware Valley other than here, I'm good." She took another sip of her drink. "That's enough about him. Tell me how your family is."

For most of the next hour he entertained her with stories about the antics of his nieces and nephews and they talked about their jobs. Then, looking at his watch and their empty glasses, he said, "We've got time for a short refill. Want me to pour?"

"We may need more ice." She went to the bar and checked. "If you'll get some, I'll pour. It's down the hall to the right," she said as she handed him the ice bucket.

After he left, she propped the door open, dumped the melting ice out of their glasses and pulled out the Scotch bottle. When he returned, she heard the door close and felt him come up behind her.

"You shouldn't leave a hotel door open like that, Margo. It's not safe." He rested his hand on her back as he reached around her to put the container on the bar.

"Oh, I'm perfectly safe," she said, tilting her head back so she could see him. "I know people in law enforcement."

"Lucky you," he said. With his forefinger he moved a few strands of hair aside and kissed her shoulder at the base of her neck. His mouth was still cool from the drink and it made her shiver. At least, that's what she blamed. At first. But when he slid his hands around her waist, and her pulse spiked, taking her breathing along for the ride, it was obvious that it wasn't just ice making her tremble. And she was sure if he did what she thought he was about to do, they'd never make it to the reunion on time.

"Maybe," she said, "we should skip the second drink and leave?" She took a deep breath and faced him. "So we're not late?" She could hear the lack of conviction in her voice and wondered if he could, too.

He touched the tip of her nose with his finger. "If that's what you want, sugar," he murmured, "we'll go." He leaned in and brushed his lips across her cheek. She was left holding an empty glass, surprised at how disappointed she was that he'd agreed and wondering why the hell she'd objected anyway.

Chapter 3

Two steps into the restaurant where the reunion dinner was being held and Margo was sure she'd gone through a time warp. The smells of tomato sauce, oregano, garlic and yeasty bread brought back long-forgotten pizza dates. Music she remembered from the senior prom was playing. The place was full of vaguely familiar-looking people with very familiar names on their nametags.

At the registration table, Joe delGiorno and Mary Margaret O'Brian delGiorno were checking people in. They'd married right after graduation and overseen every reunion, as well as a family of five kids, ever since. After Joe handed Tony his nametag and checked his name off a list, Tony asked "wine or Scotch?" and headed off for the wine she requested. Margo searched for her nametag in the middle of what was once apparently an alphabetized display, now not so organized.

"I'm sorry," Mary Margaret said, offering a marker and a blank nametag, "you'll have to make your own. Tony didn't tell us he was bringing someone."

"It's Margo Keyes, Mary Margaret."

"Oh my God! It is!" She tapped her husband's shoulder. "Joe, look. Margo's really here."

Joe came from behind the table with her nametag, gave her a hug and said, "We were so happy to hear you were coming. And you're with Tony? He never said."

"Hey, Joe, nice to see you, too. It was a last minute thing. You know, Tony and I are old friends, practically brother and sister."

"Tony's never had a brother-sister date in his life," Joe said, patting her arm. "Why would he start with you?"

Her not-so-much-brother returned and handed her a glass of

white wine. Margo began to take a gulp, but had second thoughts. Instead, she swirled the wine around in the glass, took a small sip and followed Tony inside.

The cocktail hour was winding down as people began to find seats for dinner. Thanks to her date, the basketball-star/class-officer, Margo, the newspaper-editor/head-of-the-debate-team, was at a table with people she'd never hung out with in high school: the head cheerleader, the football quarterback, the class president, the prom queen. She was back in the high school cafeteria, except this time she was at the table with the cool kids.

Seeing classmates after fifteen years wasn't as hard as she'd feared. Everyone asked about Portland. There were no awkward mentions of her father or the disaster he'd caused in her life. And, perhaps more immediately important, no one commented on Tony having his arm around her or the back of her chair any time he wasn't actually eating his dinner. At the moment, Margo was more relieved about not having to explain that.

After the tables were cleared, a DJ played more music so they could dance. However, after a couple fast dances, a slow song came on and he started toward the table.

"Let's sit this one out," he said, rather abruptly, it seemed to Margo.

"Something wrong?"

"No, I'd like to wait for a song I like better."

She thought she saw him glance across the room where his former fiancée and her husband were doing what, apparently, passed for dancing with them. And because what was playing had all the earmarks of an "our song," Margo figured she knew why they were sitting it out. On an impulse, she reached for his hands. "Maybe it's time you disconnected the song from her."

"That's not it," he started. A look that somehow combined irritation and amusement played across his face. When he raised an eyebrow, his expression went completely to amused.

"On second thought, do you think you and that dress could do something like that?"

"I'm willing to try, if you are."

He held out his arms to her, she slipped into them and he drew her close. At five-feet- seven, and in four-inch heels she almost matched his six-feet-one height. Effortlessly he moved them across the floor in time with the music. At least, she assumed the song was still playing. With his arms wrapped around her and the smell of that damn cologne filling her senses, the only thing she could really hear was the sound of his heartbeat.

After a few moments of silence, he whispered, "You were right. I'm not thinking about the song at all." His warm breath feathered over her ear, sending goose bumps down her neck to her arms and breasts.

"Good," she managed, hoping he hadn't noticed that her nipples had hardened into tight buds against his chest. She'd certainly noticed it. Just like she'd noticed the erection he had pressed against her. An erection that seemed to get harder by the second, even though it was trapped behind several layers of clothes. Clothes she was beginning to wish they could get rid of. Right now.

He slid his hand down her back; his hold tightened; her body instinctively arched toward him. Every inch of her body was aware of every inch of his. How was it possible to be so close to him and not stumble over his feet? Or—an even better question—how was it possible not to completely melt from the sheer pleasure of having his hard, muscled body pressed so tightly against her soft breasts and hips?

"This dress," he said, "no zipper, no buttons. Are you sewn in?" He rested their clasped hands against his shoulder and with a slight increase of pressure on the small of her back led her smoothly in half-circles, first one way and then the other. It was as if they were one body, joined somehow. *Stop.* She couldn't think about having their bodies joined. Not here, not in public.

"No, I just, you know, pull it on over my head." She'd had to swallow a couple times to get enough moisture in her mouth so she could answer because all the moisture in her body had taken up residence between her legs.

In a low, husky voice he said, "Off the same way, I take it?"

Holy hell, he was not only turning her body to jelly, he was reading her mind. This was not good. At the rate they were going, they'd be making this reunion memorable for everyone there by tearing each other's clothes off on the dance floor.

Then his pager beeped.

He broke his hold to retrieve it from his jacket pocket. "Goddamn. *Figlio di puttana*," he said when he saw the number. She knew he only swore in two languages when he was really pissed.

"Work, I take it."

"What else? I'm sorry, Margo. I have to answer this. Meet you back at the table." He pulled out a cell phone and walked away, punching in a number as he went.

When he returned, the expression on his face said their evening was over before he spoke a word. They made their excuses to their classmates and headed for the valet stand to get her car.

Although she protested that he needed to get to wherever he'd been called, he insisted on walking her from the hotel garage to the door of the suite. Much to her relief, nothing was said on the way up to her room about what had happened on the dance floor.

She opened the door of her suite and started to say goodnight.

"Before I go," he interrupted, "what're your plans for the rest of your visit?"

"I'm at a conference for most of the week, then a couple days hanging out before I go home." Somehow, changing her reservation to an earlier flight had slipped off her "to do" list.

"Why don't I make dinner for you at my apartment next Friday to make up for our short evening tonight?" He reached over and picked something she couldn't see off the top of her dress where it skimmed one breast. Her skin retained the heat from his fingers when he moved his hand.

"Oh," she said, "you cook."

"My mom taught us all to cook, you know that."

"Right. I forgot." She glanced down, then back at him. "What about our mothers?"

"I didn't plan on inviting them, sugar." His smile almost melted the heels on her shoes.

"I didn't mean that. It's just that if either of them knew we were having dinner in your apartment we'd never . . . I'd never . . . hear the end of it."

From the half-smile on his face, he was enjoying the conversation way too much. "As far as I can tell, the neighborhood grapevine doesn't extend to this part of the city but I appreciate you trying to protect my reputation."

She gave him what she hoped was a withering look. "It's not you I'm worried about."

With an expression still too amused for her comfort, he asked. "So, is that a yes or a no?"

"If you're sure, I guess dinner at your place would be okay." She realized how tentative that sounded and backtracked. "I mean, it sounds good. Should I give you my cell number? Or you can leave a message here for me if you have to make a change. I'm at the Convention Center all next week."

"That's where your conference is?"

"Yeah, I'm doing a presentation with some police captain on 'Law and Order' . . . "

He laughed, then asked, "'Law and Order: The Working Relationship Between the Police and the DA's Office'? I won't have to leave a message anywhere. I can hand it to you while we're standing at the podium."

"What're you talking about?" she asked.

"We're doing that presentation—you and me."

"How come I didn't know this?"

"No idea. About five days ago, the captain scheduled to be the speaker had to cancel. For reasons I have yet to be told, I got tagged. But I thought I was with a *guy* from the West Coast."

"Jeff Wyatt, my boss, was supposed to do it. But his trial ran long so he asked me to pinch-hit for him. That's how I ended up with ten days here. What do you plan to say, anyway?"

"Not sure yet. Maybe we should work on it together. How about we have lunch or something tomorrow and figure it out? About ten?"

"Ten sounds good. Don't push yourself if you have a long night. I'm around all day."

"Great." He bracketed her face with his hands and brought his mouth to hers. His lips were soft and warm, the kiss the same. But when he circled her waist with his arms and she sank into his embrace, her muscles seemed to dissolve, out of her control, as she molded herself against him and he deepened the kiss. She didn't resist when he brushed her mouth with the tip of his tongue, letting him explore the inside of her mouth at his leisure. Then he slowly drew back, until he was kissing her gently again. He ended with a kiss on the tip of her nose.

"See you tomorrow, counselor," he said as he walked down the hall toward the steps.

Chapter 4

The sound was annoying. How could she stop it? She had to swim up through the music and leave the dance and . . .

Oh, hell. The bedside clock came into view as she woke. It was ten o'clock. She'd overslept. Again. And she didn't have to guess who was at the other end of the ringing phone.

After she apologized to him and hung up, she grabbed her robe and drew it on as she ran to open the door where she found Tony putting a cell phone into the pocket of his jeans. From his damp hair, he wasn't long out of the shower and the clean-guy smell of freshly laundered shirt, some kind of sandlewood-y soap and maybe his shaving gel was almost as sexy as last night's cologne. A carrier holding two paper cups was on the floor.

He picked up the carrier and walked in. "I brought you a latte. Figured you're now one of those West Coast coffee snobs. But from the look of you I should have brought Theresa instead."

"I'm so sorry, Tony. I don't know what's going on. This is the second morning I've overslept and I never oversleep. Never." She took the cup he offered and inhaled a slug of coffee. "Thank you for this. It's just what I . . . " She stopped. "Bring Theresa? Your sister?"

"Yeah, the one who owns a salon."

She put a hand up to her hair and realized that she desperately needed a brush.

"Oh, God, I'm a mess. Here," she handed the cup back to him and headed for the bedroom. "I'll be ready in half an hour, I swear."

"Half an hour would be great. I said I'd be in before eleven to finish up some paperwork from last night before we eat. Hope you don't mind."

"Of course not. Make yourself at home. TV's over . . . " she said gesturing toward an armoire, which he was already opening. "Oh, good. You found it."

As she pushed the door shut, she heard the crack of a bat hitting a ball. If he'd found a Phillies game, she had lots of time.

Fifteen minutes later, out of the shower and wrapped in a towel, her hair brushed and twisted up with a clip, she was pulling clothes out of drawers, trying to decide what to wear. There was a tap on the door and Tony said, "Coffee's getting cold. Want it while you get ready?"

"Yes, but hold on a minute," she answered and looked around for her robe. She had only just found it under a pile of rejected outfits when the door swung open and he walked in, her cup of coffee in his hand. She clutched at the front of the towel, holding it close to her breasts.

He stopped halfway across the room. "Sweet Jesus, Margo," he said. After looking at her for a few seconds, he crossed the rest of the way to where she stood and set the coffee on a table. He'd apparently seen what he wanted to see on her face because he drew her close. As their mouths met, her hands slid up his arms and around his neck.

Margo had tried to confine her memory of kissing Tony to that inaccessible place in her mind where she kept the details of the periodic table of elements and the family tree of Elizabeth the First of England, things she needed out of her consciousness for one reason or another. She always failed. The symbol for plutonium or the name of Henry the Seventh's mother she had to work at recalling. But not Tony's kisses.

He started soft and slow, and let the kiss build in intensity seemingly without any effort on his part. When he persuaded her to let him explore her mouth with his tongue, her knees slowly melted and sparks showered through her, burning away the memory of any other man she'd ever kissed. By the time he ended the kiss—and it was always Tony who ended the kiss—she had temporarily forgotten how to breathe on her own and needed his arms to hold her upright.

He had just hooked his fingers into the top of the towel she was wearing when his pager beeped.

This time he swore only in English. "Damn it to hell," he said under his breath. He shook his head, kissed her forehead and walked out of the room to answer the page, firmly closing the door behind him.

Margo stood in the middle of the floor for a long moment, apparently incapable of movement. Eventually feeling returned to her limbs and she was able to gulp down the coffee and get dressed. Ten minutes later, she stood at the closed door of the bedroom ready to go out to the living room. A couple deep breaths and she opened the door.

She didn't know what she expected to find but it wasn't a TV on mute and Tony still on the phone, his face all business. He mouthed, "one minute," and held up his hand.

When he was finished the call he apologized. "Sorry. I asked Isaiah Bryant who caught the case to page me if he got anything more about last night."

"What *was* last night, anyway?"

"Couple found a body in the Tinicum Marsh."

"But you're not working homicide."

"Yeah, but we think this guy has a connection with someone this task force I'm on has been tracking for months. The vic had his business card in his wallet. What's interesting to us is that the vic—his name is Frank Jameson—works for Microsoft and we've been working on a series of high-tech intellectual property thefts."

"How the hell did he wind up in the Tinicum Marsh? And what was the couple doing there at that hour of the night?"

"Can't answer the first question yet. You can guess the answer to the second." His grin was positively lascivious. "They literally tripped over him under a pile of leaves and tree limbs. We're sure he was killed there, but didn't get much else from the scene. There was no luggage. No car. Only thing they found in the leaves was a boarding pass for a business class seat on a flight from Portland to Philly on Friday."

"That must have been my flight. There aren't that many flights from Portland. And I was in business class. What'd he look like?"

"Five feet ten, two-hundred-seventy pounds. Light brown hair. License says he's fifty-one. Navy blue jacket, light blue Polo shirt, khaki pants."

"Holy shit, Tony. That sounds like the Asshole in the Blue Blazer."

*

The atmosphere at the Roundhouse, Philly's distinctive double-circle-shaped police headquarters was much like the Portland Police Bureau headquarters, with which Margo was familiar. There were rows of government-issued desks covered in computers, stacks of files and reams of paper, multiple phones were ringing and, most noticeable of all, there was an overwhelming air of testosterone in spite of all the women who worked there. The only thing different was that Philly's headquarters, like its City Hall and its police force, was much bigger.

Tony walked to a desk next to a window that looked out toward the Parkway and pulled up a chair for her.

"How'd a new detective rate a window, Tony?" she asked as she sat down.

"My boyish charm?" he said.

"You're still getting the biggest piece of birthday cake, I see. Must have a woman assigning desks."

"Jesus, you sound like Theresa. We were six years old. Let it go."

"We were seven and you got a huge slice of chocolate cake and twice the ice cream the rest of us got at Jennifer's party because you batted your big brown eyes at her mother. Which I've seen you do since you were in diapers, Alessandro, and . . ."

"If you've known him that long, let me buy you a cup of coffee some day," a baritone voice interrupted from behind her.

"That invitation to tell stories about me, Margo, came from Isaiah Bryant. Isaiah, Margo Keyes, an old friend from the neighborhood. She knows as many stories about me as my sisters do and since I can't sic my mother on her, she's more likely to tell them. This may be the closest I let you two get."

She swiveled in the chair to find a tall African-American man, probably in his late forties, with café au lait skin, brown eyes, a friendly open face and, she discovered when they shook hands, a good handshake.

"Nice to meet you. Sorry Tony dragged you in here to listen to our shop talk."

"She's a DA, Isaiah. She loves this shit. And she might be able to connect that boarding pass with our vic. She thinks she got up close and personal with him in the airport."

"Actually, if it's who I think it is, I heard him on a cell phone in Portland, we got into an argument just after we landed here, and we ran into each other again at luggage pickup when I bumped him with my suitcase."

"Any idea what the phone conversation was about?" Isaiah asked.

"Sounded like he was negotiating with someone, trying to sell them something. He said, 'I know someone who'll buy it if you won't.' And, 'What're you willing to pay me for it? I'll call you when I hear what he has to say.' Or something along those lines."

"No indication what he was selling?" Tony asked.

"Nope. And whatever it was, I'm not sure he had it with him, unless it was small enough to fit in his briefcase."

"Briefcase? We didn't find a briefcase at the scene," Bryant said.

"Well, he had one when he left the airport. It was sitting in front of me when I pulled my bag off the luggage belt," Margo said. "He grabbed it and ran to the taxi stand."

"I'll have someone go back and hunt through the leaves again. And what you saw confirms what we suspected—there was no car there so we assumed, unless the perp drove him, he took a cab. Been contacting taxi companies. I'll ask about a briefcase. Maybe Jameson left it in a cab," Bryant said. "But it's more likely the shooter took it."

After she'd identified the body as her guy in the blue blazer, Margo dictated a statement, and then eavesdropped as Bryant told Tony what he'd gotten from a Microsoft contact in Redmond, Washington.

According to the man he'd talked to, Frank Jameson had been in software development for Microsoft since he'd graduated from college. When Bryant contacted Jameson's wife—or more accurately, he discovered, the wife from whom Jameson had recently separated—she said he had called on Wednesday to cancel a camping trip with their sons for business reasons. She added they should talk to his girlfriend for more information, and she gave him a phone number.

The girlfriend confirmed Jameson was away on a business trip. He'd called after he arrived at his destination, although he hadn't told her where he was. She'd tried his cell phone a number of times but it always went to voice mail. She planned to give him hell for worrying her when he returned Sunday afternoon.

Chapter 5

Tony and Margo's presentation was scheduled for late in the afternoon on Thursday, giving them four days to pull it together. During their brainstorming session on Sunday, Tony started off with a couple ideas he "just wanted to throw out." When he outlined the ideas, Margo decided he just wanted to make her laugh.

First, he suggested using the theme from the television show *Law & Order* as they walked to the podium, or to imitate the "chung, CHUNG" sound the show used to switch scenes when they changed speakers. She assured him they were great ideas, but unfortunately, she didn't have time to acquire the rights for public performance and had to veto them.

Next, he moved to a list of specific police and lawyer TV shows he thought they could recommend. Since, he said, he was sure the lawyer shows were as accurate as the cop shows were, watching them would be helpful in understanding how the entire justice system worked. She asked how the hell he had time to watch so much television when he was a working detective. However, she added, since he was headed in that direction, maybe there was a way they could play the opening for laughs and she outlined an idea he readily accepted.

Before she took off for her mother's, Tony asked if they could spend part of each of the following days working on the presentation. Margo quickly agreed. After all, that would make their speeches better. The fact that it meant they would be together every day was incidental. Wasn't it?

Monday they got the opening scripted during lunch at the Reading Terminal Market, the mother of all farmers' markets, and Margo's favorite source of sticky buns and cheese steaks. Tuesday they had drinks after work at a little neighborhood bar near his apartment where she met several of his colleagues and his favorite bartender. Over glasses of wine, they discussed their personal experiences, developing a list of the points they wanted to emphasize and examples they could use to illustrate them.

When she'd casually mentioned on Tuesday that she'd never ridden on a motorcycle, Tony picked her up at the end of the day on Wednesday so he could take her for a tour of Fairmount Park on the back of his bike. After an hour's ride, they parked and walked through the sculpture garden, rehearsing. By the time he delivered her back to her hotel, they were both satisfied with the information they were presenting.

All week she looked forward to seeing him, saving up stories and nuggets of information from the conference to share with him. They didn't revisit the heat they'd generated on the dance floor or in her hotel room that Sunday but he always seemed to have his arm around her, or his hand on hers. He kissed her hello and goodbye, sometimes kissed her just because. And she loved holding him so tight her fingers cramped as they took the corners of the winding roads in the park on his motorcycle. If they'd had more time, she thought, maybe . . .

She was sure as hell in no hurry for Thursday to arrive.

But arrive it did. As they got to the meeting room where they were scheduled to present, she hesitated outside the door. "I'm nervous about pulling this off, Tony. We've really only had two run-throughs of the whole thing. That's not a lot of practice."

He opened the door and waved her into the room. "It's show time, counselor. You'll do fine."

They began with Tony.

"Working with Deputy District Attorney Keyes to get this presentation organized was a pleasure. Although she's now in Portland, Oregon, we grew up next door to each other here in

Philadelphia. We've always had great personal and professional respect for each other so . . . "

The blast of a whistle interrupted.

Tony turned in the direction of the sound. Margo was sitting at the end of the table, a Police Athletic League lanyard around her neck and the whistle at the end of the lanyard in her mouth. "Margo," he said in a stage whisper, "what are you doing?"

She took the whistle from her mouth and smiled sweetly. "You told me to be timekeeper. Your time's up."

He looked at his watch. "But we have ninety minutes."

"Didn't you get my memo about this?"

"A memo?"

"Yeah, you know, paperwork." She pulled a three-inch thick sheaf of papers out of her messenger bag. "You said you should go first because that's how the system works—we bat cleanup after you guys have done all the hard work—and I could be the timekeeper. It's all in here." She pushed the stack of papers toward him and he picked it up.

"*This* is your memo?"

"Well, the memo is the first three pages. The rest is my presentation."

He threw the pile of papers onto the table in front of him. "Lawyers and their damn paperwork," he said with disgust.

She joined him at the podium. "Cops who fly by the seat of their pants," she said and rolled her eyes.

When the laughter died down, they began the real presentation, focusing on how to make the relationship between the two halves of the criminal justice system more productive. They were a hit, mostly because they talked about what worked well and emphasized how to effect change in their own organizations. And the introduction making light of the stereotypes of each of their professions had entertained everyone.

At the end of the session, after an extended round of applause, they were about to leave when a woman approached and put her arms out to Margo for a hug.

"Margo Keyes! Who knew you were such a good actress?"

Margo returned the gesture. "Beth Dahl. I thought that was you in the back of the room. It's been ages." She started to introduce her co-presenter, but was interrupted.

"Hey, Beth," Tony said. "How do you two know each other?"

"Law school," the two women said at once.

"And how do you know each other?" Margo asked.

"DA's office," Tony and Beth said in unison.

Tony looked across the room. "You two have a mini-Berkeley reunion. I see someone I want to say hi to before I leave. Walk you back to your hotel, Margo?"

"Sure. Just give me five minutes." She watched him walk across the room then turned her attention back to her classmate. "How long have you been in the DA's office here?"

"Two years. Been a great experience for a kid from Kansas."

"I imagine." She looked over Beth's shoulder at Tony, deep in conversation with two uniformed police officers. "Have you heard from anyone . . . ?"

Beth interrupted. "Margo, do you know about the Blue Flu?"

Surprised at the change of topic, Margo looked quizzically at her classmate. "You mean cops calling in sick when they want to protest?"

"We have another disease here. The Alessandro Virus. It infects women exposed to Tony. It's practically epidemic. Or is it endemic? Pandemic? Whatever, it looks like you have a bad case of it."

Margo protested, "We're just old friends."

"Not from what I'm seeing. You look at him like he's some chocolate dessert and you haven't had sweets since the beginning of Lent."

"Really, just long-time friends. Honestly." Margo wondered if her nose was growing.

"Do long-time friends have insights into why a straight, gorgeous, smart cop who has no problems working with women doesn't ever get personally involved with one?"

"Maybe Nicole burned him worse than I heard." She hastened to explain. "She's the ex-fiancée who left him for another guy."

"Stupid woman." Beth cocked her head and smiled. "There couldn't be somebody, maybe not in Philly, who's standing in the way of local talent getting his attention, could there?"

Margo looked her classmate in the eye. "Sorry, Beth, I don't know."

"Yeah, I bet." Beth was smirking and Margo was trying as hard as she could to keep her expression neutral.

The subject of their conversation returned and they moved on to safer—at least in Margo's opinion—subjects. After promising to keep in touch, Margo hugged Beth again and headed to the elevator with Tony.

"So," he said, "you know Beth. She's built a good reputation in a short time." He punched the button to call the elevator.

"Of course she's good. You get great lawyers from Berzerk-ly."

"What were you two talking about so intently? Didn't know law school gossip was that interesting."

"Nothing much. Just what she was doing here." She hit the button a couple more times. Unable to get the elevator to provide a diversion, she changed the direction of the conversation. "We kicked ass in our presentation today." Margo put up her hand for a high-five. "We were much better than any of the other speakers I've heard this week."

He touched the palm of her hand with the flat of his. "I'm shocked, counselor, *shocked* to find out you're so competitive."

"Yeah, it's a recent development in my personality."

Tony laughed. "But you said you were nervous. If that was nervous, I hope to hell I never have to work with you when you're confident. No one would notice I was in the room."

"Thanks." She looked up at him. "That was a compliment, wasn't it?" Before he could answer she said, "Never mind, I'm taking it as one."

The elevator arrived and he held the door open for her to enter. "Have dinner with me at our table tonight?"

"I promised Danny Hartmann and Greer Payne I'd join them."

"Who're they? I've never heard you talk about him—her—them before, have I?"

"Both are shes. Danny's a Portland detective, a good one, and Greer's another deputy DA. Also a good one."

"At least let me walk you back to the Convention Center."

"Sounds like a plan." The elevator stopped and they went out into the late afternoon sun. When they reached her hotel, they agreed to meet in the lobby at six.

Once in her room Margo took advantage of the time difference to call Portland and catch up on how her cases were doing. Just before she was due to meet Tony, she exchanged the tailored jacket of her black suit for a white camisole and black and white silk kimono jacket, the bottom of which she tied loosely around her waist. She put on silver hoop earrings and the Manolo Blahniks. A few minutes before six, she went down to the lobby.

He was waiting for her in a re-run of the Saturday night before, down to the Italian loafers and the spicy cologne he'd splashed on after shaving again. And like that night, he took her breath away. If only the week wasn't just about over.

The unexpected reception they got at the cocktail party was as close to rock star level as either of them was ever likely to experience. Word of their entertaining presentation had apparently spread to those who hadn't been in the room and multiple hugs, handshakes and words of congratulation were offered.

Then Greer Payne arrived. As was always the case, when Greer walked into a room, all eyes—at least the eyes of all the males—

turned to her. No matter how many times she saw it, Margo felt all the air go out of her tires when it happened.

It's not that Margo didn't respect her colleague's skills. She did. The way she felt about Greer was more personal. There was Greer's laugh that was so completely, flawlessly ladylike; the sound of a crystal bell, really. Then there was the perfectly coiffed blonde hair, the carefully manicured nails, the stylish clothes that always looked impeccable. Greer could make Margo feel rumpled and grubby simply by walking into the room.

As she did tonight. She wore a black linen, V-necked, sleeveless sheath, emphasizing every curve in her well-toned body, with not one wrinkle in it. Didn't the woman ever sit? A fine gold chain dangled a tastefully sized but-still-large-enough-to-make-you-look diamond just above her cleavage, which could be described exactly the same way.

"Margo, there you are." Greer had worked her way across the room, fending off drink offers and dinner invitations. "I heard good things about your presentation today. Jeff will be happy he picked you to sub for him, won't he?"

"Thanks, Greer. I hope he will, yes."

Greer raked Tony from head to toe with her big, green, artfully made-up eyes, like a cat eyeing a tuna steak. She put her hand out. "Hello, I'm Greer Payne."

Margo finished the introduction.

"Oh, you were Margo's partner today, weren't you? No wonder she did such a good job. She must have wanted to impress you, too."

"She did that a long time ago," Tony said. "When we were kids she learned to ride a bike before I did. Impressed the hell out of me." He grinned at Margo who smiled at the memory.

"You've known each other that long? Isn't she lucky?" Greer had yet to release Tony's hand. Without breaking eye contact with him, she said, "Are you ready for dinner, Margo? They're asking us to move to our tables. Please join us, Tony."

"Thanks, but I'm committed. And Margo, can we finish what we were talking about before you go?"

Margo waited until her colleague had left then said, "What were we talking about?"

"Nothing. But I wanted to ask you to have a nightcap with me at your hotel when this is all over."

"I'd love to. I'll even buy to thank you for waiting until Greer was gone to ask. Otherwise I'd be buying for her, too."

"Is she that close a friend that she'd expect to be included?"

"Oh, yeah. She's a big fan." She paused for a beat. "Of good-looking men. I bet she could describe what you're wearing down to your socks and underwear, but wouldn't have any idea what I have on."

Tony cocked his head and furrowed his brow. "I've never heard you talk about another woman like that."

"When I'm around her I feel like changing everything about me and putting her in some kind of plastic bag."

"Don't do either. I like you the way you are and if you got caught stuffing her into a body bag I'd have to come see you in prison. I don't like visiting people in prison."

She smiled. "I'll keep that in mind."

Following the predictable-but-not-too-boring speeches, Margo said good night to her dinner companions and headed for the back of the room to wait for Tony. Before she got there, she felt a hand at the small of her back. She didn't bother to look around. "Where is it, Tony?"

"Where's what, Margo?" It sounded like he was suppressing a laugh as he said it.

"I don't know—GPS? Cell phone tap? You must have something on me to know when I left the table."

"Sorry, it's on a need-to-know-basis. And you don't . . . "

"Yeah, yeah, yeah. I don't need to know."

Chapter 6

Margo ordered a Brandy Alexander and Tony a Tuaca. When the drinks arrived, Tony lifted his glass. "*Salute*. It's been a great week."

Margo touched her glass to his. "It's been fun doing this with you. Thank you."

"And thank you for ordering a drink in my honor."

She shot him a puzzled look, then got it. "Oh, right. Brandy Alessandro. This is my favorite after-dinner drink. Never made the connection with your family."

"Sure it's my family?" He leaned closer to her, his brown eyes almost black in the dimly lit bar, and took her free hand with his.

She smiled. "I wouldn't think you'd have to stoop to angling for a compliment. Don't you still have to beat women off with a stick?"

"Funny how that works. The one you want to hang around moves a continent away. The ones who stay, you don't care about."

Greer Payne materialized at the table, interrupting what was working into an interesting conversation, a man in tow who she failed to introduce. "Hello, Tony, nice to see you. And Margo—are you staying here, too? I thought you'd be home. With your mother."

Margo pulled her hand away from Tony and moved a bit to put some space between them. "Portland's home, Greer, and, yes, I'm staying here." She took a deep breath and tried to be more pleasant. "I didn't have a chance at dinner to ask if you've gotten out to see much of Philly."

"A little bit. What would you recommend I see, Tony?" The green eyes she turned to him seemed to shine in the dim light, as did the gold in her hair.

"You really shouldn't miss the Liberty Bell and Independence Hall." He finished his drink. "I hate to recommend and run, but we were just about to leave. Do you and your, ah, friend want the booth?"

"Thanks, but we're meeting people. Do you have to leave? I was hoping you'd join us."

"*We'd* like to but I have an early morning tomorrow," Tony said as he stood up. He put out a hand to assist Margo in getting out of the booth.

It took all of Margo's considerable determination to keep from laughing as they left the bar. She gave into it as soon as they were out the door. "The Liberty Bell and Independence Hall? Jesus, Tony, how obvious could you be that you were brushing her off?"

He flashed a wicked, conspiratorial grin. "And she didn't even break stride when I did it. It was time to get out of there anyway so I could walk you to your room."

"You don't have to . . . "

"Are you using your skills at brushing men off or shall we grab an elevator?"

She looked up at him as she linked her arm through his and could tell from his expression he knew what her answer was.

The elevator arrived and, when they got on, he draped his arm around her shoulder. She moved close to him, nestled in the circle of his arm, waiting for the kiss she was sure was coming. Instead, he said, "I'm not ready to end the evening. Okay if I come in for a while?"

"I'd love it." She put her hand on his chest.

The door closed and she got the kiss she wanted. Her hands went to his shoulders; his slid down her back and pulled her close. His mouth sweet from the Tuaca, he tasted better than anything she'd ever had and she sipped her fill. As his tongue made love to her mouth, expertly exploring every inch of it, she began to lose control of her breathing and her legs got all rubbery.

The elevator door opening interrupted them. She backed away from Tony as if hit with a cattle prod. A man got on, nodded good evening to them and punched the button for the sixth floor. With a distinctive English accent he said, "May I assist with the button for your floor?"

Embarrassed they'd forgotten, Margo said in a weak voice, "Eight, please."

In silence, they rode up to the sixth floor. When the door opened, the Englishman nodded and said, "Have a good evening. Although I rather doubt you need my encouragement to do so." Margo burst into laughter as the door closed.

She was still laughing when they reached the eighth floor. Tony laced his fingers through hers as they walked to her suite. She'd never imagined how sexy handholding could be but walking with her hand wrapped in his stronger, bigger one as he slowly rubbed his thumb over hers was almost as exciting as having him hold her in his arms.

As she dug in her purse for the key card, he said, "This has a vaguely familiar feel to it. That summer, after graduation, we'd come home from the shore, sit in that old car of my dad's down the block making out for a while, then go up to your house, like we just walked down the hall. You'd fish out your keys, like you're doing now. Your mom was always waiting for you."

"Ah, there's the difference," she said. "No one's waiting inside here. I've outgrown the need to have someone protect my virtue."

"I'm in luck, then." Tangling his fingers in her hair, he drew her mouth to his. The kiss was soft but it lingered, suggesting he wanted more. When they separated, she tried to get the door open but her hand was shaking. He took the key card from her, unlocked the door and pushed it open. She went to the bar, turned to ask what he wanted to find he was only inches away, his hands reaching for her.

"I don't want a drink," he said, as if reading her thoughts. "And I'm done with conversation for the evening. I'm looking at what

I want." He took her hand and pressed a kiss into the palm. She swore she could feel the kiss in every part of her body. "The money question, sugar, is what do *you* want?"

Circling his neck with her arms, she brought her mouth to his. She left the sweet kiss in the hall. Distilling a week of touching him, having his arm around her, his eyes on her into one kiss, she made a blazingly passionate connection with his mouth and his body. She tasted every inch of his mouth then teased his lips open so she could play hide and seek with his tongue.

"Are we on the same page?" she asked, pulling back from him and looking into his chocolate eyes, now dark with desire.

"I'm not sure. Let's try that again." He pulled her back to him and returned the kiss with equal urgency, demanding a response from her mouth, from her body, making her dizzy with longing. "I think we're okay," he said in a husky voice. He ran his hands around to her back, pulled her hips tight against him. The hard length of his erection pressed against her and her body responded to his with a wave of warmth that centered low in her belly. She wanted to rub herself all over him, purring, like a cat.

Trying to take a breath, to slow down the pace at which she was turning to warm, sweet honey in his arms, she put her head back. But it didn't help. Now with access to her throat, he started along her jaw line and kissed his way to the rapidly beating pulse there. Then he nibbled at her neck and back up to her ear. She was drowning in wanting him.

She didn't feel him undo it but suddenly her jacket was slithering off her shoulders and down her hips to the floor. His hands caressed her through the thin silk camisole, circling her nipples, making her gasp with pleasure. Her breasts ached to feel his bare hands. She wanted to touch his skin. She pushed his jacket over his shoulders and he shrugged it off while she fumbled with the buttons on his shirt, her fingers having trouble with the simple task of pushing a small white button through a buttonhole.

"Should we . . . ?" he started.

" . . . go in there," she finished. She wasn't sure she could actually walk to take him to her bed.

He solved the problem. "I've always wanted to do this," he said, picking her up as though she were a tiny thing, carrying her into the bedroom, setting her gently down on the bed.

In the shadow-dimmed room, he unzipped her skirt and helped her shimmy out of it. She pulled the camisole over her head and he unhooked her bra with one flick of his fingers, sliding the straps off her shoulders, adding it to the skirt on the floor.

He stood up to finish the job she'd started of unbuttoning his shirt. Scooting over into the middle of the bed, she settled back onto a pillow, her head resting on one arm.

On a sharp intake of breath, he said, "God, you're beautiful."

Embarrassed, she began to pull on the hem of the sheet the maid had turned down.

"Don't do that, sugar, please. Let me look at you, at all of you."

Reluctantly, she dropped the sheet, leaving most of her body exposed. The intensity of his gaze made her self-conscious at first. Then she got lost in watching him undress, lit from the light coming in from the living room.

His handsome face was soft with desire; the sculpted muscles in his arms and shoulders, the flat stomach he was gradually uncovering were like the cover of a romance novel or a really, really good fantasy. She'd seen him in cutoffs and bathing trunks and knew he had a magnificent body, but she'd always wondered where that line of hair led that started in the dark hair dusting his chest. Now she knew. It ended in a nest of dark curls from the middle of which sprung the impressive erection she'd felt against her. The erection that would soon be pressed against her again, would soon be inside her. Her fingers curled into the palms of her hand, wanting to touch the soft hair, his rock-hard penis. At just the thought, her breathing became faster, more ragged.

Before he joined her, he took condoms out of the back pocket of his trousers and flipped one onto the bed next to her. Once beside her, he began to slowly explore her body with his hands and his mouth, moving from her face down her throat on his way to her breasts. "I've never forgotten what you tasted like right here," he licked and nipped softly at the base of her throat, "that summer after a day in the sun." He kissed between her breasts. "You tasted like the ocean."

With his tongue, he circled the nipple of one breast, raking his teeth across the sensitive skin, contracting it into a small, hard point. When she moaned and her body pushed toward him, he moved to the other breast and gave it similar attention. Her breasts felt full, heavy, aching for more of his mouth, his hands.

"I wanted to do this that summer but I didn't think you'd let me. I thought about it every time we were together."

"I'd never have . . . " She moaned again and she arched her back to get more of her breast closer to his mouth. "If you'd . . . I couldn't have . . . I was afraid." The confession came out on a ragged breath.

"But not tonight?"

"Tonight, I want you to do everything, anything."

With his hands—oh, God, his hands—he trailed heat from her breasts back to her face and then to her belly. Every place he touched was on fire. He took his time with each move, giving her a chance to say no. Not that she did. She never would. Not when it felt like this, when the kisses that followed each new touch soothed what he'd inflamed. Not when she loved the taste of his mouth, the pressure of his hands.

When he came back to her lips, he hesitated, caressing her mouth with his thumbs, her eyebrows and cheekbones with his fingers, as if creating a tactile memory in his hands. "You're so beautiful. These mysterious blue eyes," he kissed each eyelid. "This cute nose," he dropped a kiss on the tip of it. "A mouth I can't stay away from." A mouth he took possession of in a way that left her wanting more when he ended it, more of his mouth, more of his hands, more of his body. She wanted to tell him he was beautiful, too, but she couldn't make her mouth form words.

All she could do was explore his body as he was exploring hers, feeling the soft hair on his chest, the pebbly texture of his nipples, the firm muscles that lay under the smooth skin on his shoulders and upper arms, his flat abs, the soft tip of his steely shaft with a drop of moisture on it. His heart pounded against her; her heartbeat answered.

He shifted her to her back, then eased his fingers under the edge of her bikini panties, feeling his way to the delta of curls between her thighs. She helped him push the panties over her hips and down off her legs, tangling in the sheets as she did. She impatiently kicked at them.

"It's okay. I want this too but we don't need to hurry," he murmured.

Then he touched her, just touched her, in the place between her thighs where all the heat from his caresses had pooled and the sheets didn't matter anymore. She saw stars. When his soft caress became more urgent, her hips bucked toward him as he slipped one finger, then two, inside her, moving in and out as his thumb circled her clitoris.

"Come for me, sugar. Don't hold back," he whispered.

She couldn't even if she wanted. And she didn't want to. Wave after wave of bliss carried her over the edge, her body clamping hard on his fingers. "Oh, Tony, I . . ." The rest was lost as the world around dissolved, leaving only the two of them and the intense feeling that washed over her.

"That's my girl," he said, his voice raspy with desire. "My sweet, sweet, sugar." He quickly covered himself, insinuated one of his legs between hers and pressed himself against her thigh as she rocked her hips against him. She buried her fingers in his hair and pulled his mouth to hers. He entered her slowly, stretching her to accommodate him. She wrapped one leg around his waist and tilted her hips against him.

"Please, Tony, I want all of you."

"I don't want to hurt you. You feel so tight." On a groan, he said, "You feel so good." He pulled her other leg around him, controlling both of them until he was totally and completely inside her. Then he matched the rhythm of his tongue with the rhythm of his hips, moving with her, letting her set the pace as she ground her hips against him, rubbing her clitoris against his pelvis. She felt herself begin to climax again and as her insides clamped around him, he thrust into her hard and fast, taking her with him, moving them up the steep curve of passion as they climbed together over the edge of the cliff they'd been walking along for days.

Afterwards, they lay facing each other as she traced around his eyes and mouth with languid fingers and he nibbled at her hand. The expression on his face was one she'd never seen, in spite of all the years she'd known him. It was tender, affectionate, maybe . . . maybe what? It couldn't be anything more than being caught up in the moment. Could it? She wanted to know. "Tony, what . . . ?"

There must have been something in her voice that gave her away; his expression changed as if she'd used a remote to flip the channel. In place of the expression she didn't recognize was the seductive smile of the Tony she'd known all her life. She wondered if what she thought she saw was only a trick of light.

He gently kissed her forehead and whispered, "So, the girl-next-door is not only beautiful and smart but very, very sexy."

She paused for a beat or two, trying to understand what was going on, finally deciding to follow him in playing it lightly. "And the boy-next-door is as good at everything else as he is at kissing." When she moved to cuddle into him, she felt something crinkle under her. She rummaged around and brought out the empty condom wrapper, presenting it to him like it was Exhibit A. "And he's always prepared, apparently."

He laughed. "I'll take care of it," and headed for the bathroom.

When he got back in bed, he pulled her close against him, his expression still inscrutable.

"If I'd known how the week was going to end I might not have dreaded the trip so much," she said.

"Surely after Mary Ellen's wedding you could see this coming, pardon the pun. Aren't you the girl who's smarter than the teachers?"

"Terrible pun and what do you mean, 'smarter than the teachers'?"

He turned her onto her back and began kissing his way from her temple down her jaw line over her cheek to her mouth. "Isn't that what the yearbook said about you?"

She pushed him back so she could see his face. "You're joking. You looked up what was in the yearbook about me?"

"I couldn't let you get away with that embarrassing speech in front of my mother's house, could I? Took me forever to find the damn thing."

He kissed the pulse in her throat. "Smarter than most of the teachers." He returned to her mouth. "Likely to succeed at whatever she does." His hand began moving down her thigh. "'Would argue with the devil himself.' I'd say that description still works."

She grabbed his hand and held it still. "I don't argue with everyone."

"Yes, you do." His mouth found one breast. "You always have." He went to the other breast.

"No," she said, pulling back from him. "I don't."

"Is there any way I can get you to stop arguing about arguing?"

She let go of his hand and he figured it out.

*

About two A.M., he kissed her and said, "I better go."

"Can't you stay?"

"Not a good idea. You have friends around, people you work with . . . Greer."

"I thought we agreed I didn't need someone to protect my reputation anymore."

"No, we agreed you didn't need anyone looking out for your virtue. Your reputation is something else."

While he got dressed, she went into the bathroom, emerging in a hotel terry cloth robe. "Will I see you tomorrow—today—later—at the Convention Center?" she asked as she walked him to the door.

"How about breakfast at seven-thirty? I'm going to one morning session, then back to work." After she nodded agreement, he took her face in his hands, said, "I'll see you then. Sleep well, sugar," kissed her and was gone.

She slumped against the door after he'd closed it behind him and slowly slid down until she was sitting on the floor, her back to the door, her arms wrapped around her bent knees. Her lips were swollen from his kisses; her breasts tender from his mouth. She could feel his arms holding her, his body loving her. Could see the way he looked at her. How could this be? Making love with Tony? It wasn't possible. But it happened.

It took every bit of her willpower to stay on the floor when what she wanted to do was run after him and beg him to stay. She wanted him to curl around her while she slept, wanted to wake up to him the next morning.

Oh, God, what was she thinking? Obviously she needed some distance, a chance to think about this. Figure it out. She needed a good night's sleep to clear her head.

Like that was going to happen tonight.

*

He walked out onto Broad Street into the warm summer night.

He hadn't reached the first corner when he turned and started back to the hotel. He didn't care about anyone seeing him; he wanted to spend the night with her. He stopped. No, that was a very bad idea. He couldn't do that to her. He turned toward his apartment. Then he stopped again. He could be careful; no one would see him. He took two steps toward the Bellevue. Stopped again. Jesus, anyone who saw him would think he was drunk. He shook his head and some last vestige of common sense clicked into place. He couldn't go back to the hotel. Period. He strode down Broad Street in the direction of home.

At least he made one good decision tonight. He wasn't so sure about some of the others. What the hell had happened back in that hotel room? Sweet Jesus, Mother of God, he'd never been blindsided like that before. He was always the one in control of what went on with the women in his life. At least since the Nicole debacle. How could this have happened?

And with Margo. He'd known her all his life, loved her like a sister—okay, that wasn't accurate. He'd never looked at her like a sister, not since they were kids. So he cared for her, liked her a lot, they were friends, more than friends, although less than lovers. Until now. Sure, they'd dated a little, made out a lot. He'd always like kissing her, wondered what it would be like to take it further but she'd never seemed interested and that had been okay. It was complicated with all the history between their families and the three thousand miles between them.

Then at Mary Ellen's wedding, when they'd been alone in that small dark room, would have gone back to his apartment if his nephew and her mother hadn't interrupted, it seemed to change. He thought maybe she wanted it, too. So he set it up.

But what happened tonight wasn't what he'd bargained for. It blew his mind, scraped raw his emotions and opened his eyes to something he never expected to see.

So now what?

Chapter 7

"Are you by yourself? Can I join you?" Danny Hartmann asked. Margo was standing in front of the breakfast buffet, scanning the room, when the tall, blonde Portland detective found her.

"Well, I thought I might be joining a friend but it looks like I'm not. It would be nice to have company. I'd love to have breakfast with you."

Danny picked up a plate. "Were you looking for that gorgeous guy you were with last night? Who is he?"

"If you'd come to our presentation, you'd know who he is."

"I can hear you any time I want in Portland. I went to the panel on dealing with gangs."

"Any new ideas?"

"No one's having any better luck at it than we are, it sounds like." Danny loaded her plate with eggs and bacon. "But tell me about the guy. You looked too cozy in the bar last night to just be colleagues."

"We were celebrating. Got great reviews on our talk. And we're old friends."

"Friends with benefits?"

"That one over there okay with you?" Margo indicated a nearby table with her plate of bagel, cream cheese and lox before setting it down to pour coffee for herself.

"Did you hear what I asked, Margo?"

"Yes, but I don't think there's much more to get out of this line of conversation." She took a bite of her bagel. "You going to the DNA session this morning?"

Hartmann seemed to be considering whether it was worth it to pursue the subject of the gorgeous guy. She apparently decided it wasn't and answered, "Yeah, you?"

"Uh-huh, then I'm not sure what else I want to hear."

"There're a couple more that look interesting. I haven't decided. You have plans for dinner tonight?"

Margo was about to say she did when it occurred to her that Tony had never said anything more about dinner. "Not really. Want to get out of the hotel and try someplace else?"

"Always glad to get a restaurant recommendation from a native."

"About seven in the lobby, then."

The two sessions she attended that morning dragged. She couldn't concentrate on the speakers, constantly checking her phone for a text message or a voice mail. Her mother left the latter and Kiki the former, but neither was the person she wanted to hear from.

With no appetite for lunch, she left the convention center for a walk and found even the summer sun couldn't burn away the memory of the night before. She sighed. What was it he said last night—she was smart and sexy? She wasn't sure about the sexy part but she hoped she was smart enough not to read too much into what happened. Last night was about getting caught up in the mood, celebrating their good day, maybe too much to drink, which was probably what the wedding reception had been. That dance at the reunion, too. Maybe those religions that banned dancing were right. It gave you dangerous ideas.

He was her friend, like she told Beth and Danny. She was a boring lawyer who'd had her nose in one book or another all her life. He was the all-star athlete and handsomest man who'd ever walked the face of the earth. Women like her didn't get guys like Tony except maybe on occasional loan. Like from the library, when you get a copy of a best seller that you could only have for a short time because someone like Greer is waiting for it. Not only that, she has an in with the librarian and could keep renewing it until she was finished with it.

No, she had to stop thinking he'd call and want anything more than what they'd had. She'd go out to dinner with Danny and figure out later how she was going to face him over his mother's dinner table the next time she was in Philly.

When she looked up she saw that her wandering had brought her back to the Bellevue. She took that as a sign she should ditch the last afternoon of the conference and headed for her room. She'd soak in the tub. Maybe have a massage. Read a book. But before she could do any of those things she had to see why the light on her phone was flashing. The desk clerk told her she had a hand-delivered message waiting for her.

It was from Tony apologizing for missing breakfast. He'd gotten called out and by the time he'd had a chance to let her know he wouldn't make it, it was too late to leave a message at the hotel and he didn't have her cell phone number. He asked her to call to confirm seven that night for the dinner he'd promised.

He picked up on the first ring and didn't bother with hello. "Am I forgiven?"

"There's nothing to forgive. It was work. You don't owe me an explanation."

"Yes, I do. I stood you up for breakfast. So I'll make it up with dinner tonight. We didn't get around to setting a time, did we? Does seven work?" He sounded like he usually did, warm, friendly, good-guy Tony.

"Since we hadn't made definite plans I said I'd have dinner with Danny."

"You can see her when you're back in Portland. Tell her there's a change of plans."

"I hate women who break dates with their female friends as soon as the first man comes along and asks them out."

"I'm going to pretend you didn't call me 'the first man who comes along' and remind you that we had a date before you made plans with her." His voice softened. "Please, Margo. We need to talk."

Her stomach lurched. *We need to talk?* Oh, God, when was that sentence ever good? Tony wouldn't do that, would he? Or would he? What had she been telling herself all day? "Yeah, I guess we should talk."

"So, you'll come for dinner?"

"How about drinks here at the hotel. Wouldn't that be better?"

He was silent for a few moments. "No, but if that's the best I can get, it'll do. What time?"

"Six-thirty?"

"I'll be at your suite at six-thirty."

"No, not here." She couldn't bear to have him back in her room again. The space was already too full of him, his cologne, their lovemaking. "The bar downstairs."

"The bar." Another silence. "Okay, if that's what you want. See you then."

Margo called Danny and begged her forgiveness for what she was doing, explaining that she had to get something straightened out with Tony. Danny laughed and said she would run over her own mother to get something straight with Tall, Dark and Sexy.

Getting ready for their drink, she tried on every combination of clothes she had with her. Nothing seemed right. But then, she wasn't exactly sure what the appropriate dress was for meeting a man who was about to let you down gently after sleeping with you. At least she hoped it would be gently.

Finally, she settled on the gray linen pants she'd just gotten back from the hotel cleaners, the white camisole and a wide black belt that emphasized her slender waist. He might not notice how she looked but it made her more confident to feel attractive. Attractive. As she said that to herself, she heard the sharp intake of his breath as he looked at her when she was naked, when he told her how beautiful she was. The image of him standing beside the bed, half dressed, staring at her, was burned into her brain.

Oh, God, how was she going to get through the next hour?

She carefully applied make-up and lip-gloss, sprayed on perfume. On the way down to the lobby she did the deep breathing exercises she'd learned in a meditation class but only seemed to use when she was in a panic, never when she actually tried to meditate.

Hoping to be the first to arrive, she'd gone to the bar early only to find he was already there, looking good enough to eat with a spoon. How he could make ordinary black trousers and a white shirt look sexy, she didn't know but he did.

As soon as he saw her he slid out of the booth he'd claimed for them—the one they'd sat in the night before, she noticed—and stood to greet her. He flashed the glacier-melting smile but after he kissed her cheek, he frowned.

"You okay? You look . . . "

"Yes, of course I'm okay. Why wouldn't I be?" She slipped into the back of the booth, not sitting close to him, trying not to notice the question in his eyes. Two glasses, which appeared to have Scotch in them, were sitting on cocktail napkins, one at his place and the other next to him. She moved the second glass in front of her and took a large sip.

"I ordered bruschetta for you. You still like it, don't you?" he said indicating the plate with four slices of toasted bread topped with tomatoes and chopped basil.

"Yes, thanks. That was nice of you. But I'm not very hungry right now."

"How was the conference today? Go to any interesting sessions?" He picked up his glass and touched it to hers.

"Is that what you wanted to talk about?"

"No, but I thought . . . "

"Why did you say we needed to talk?"

"Okay, no small talk. Got it." He took a sip of his drink, "About last night . . . "

God, here it comes. She looked down into her glass, counting the ice cubes, which suddenly seemed of infinite interest.

"Walking home last night, I got to thinking, we made . . . well, *I* made . . . a big mistake."

"Yeah, you're probably right. Don't worry. I didn't take it seriously." She used her nail to move an ice cube around in the glass.

He frowned. "Didn't take what seriously?"

"You made a mistake. I get it. We'll just go on from here." She continued to play with the ice in her glass, avoiding his eyes, hoping he didn't see that she was beginning to tear up.

"Margo, if I promise to circle back later and try to figure out what the hell you're talking about, will you let me finish what I started to say?" He didn't wait for a response, but went on. "As I was saying, walking home I realized I made a mistake last night. I should have taken you to my place. Then I wouldn't have had to leave; you won't run into Greer or anyone else you know there. So, how about you check out of the hotel and stay at my apartment until you go back to Portland on Sunday?"

She was sure she looked as stunned as she felt.

The confident look he'd been wearing began to fade. "If you don't think it's a good idea, that's okay. I mean, you were worried about our families knowing about dinner so maybe you won't want to stay with me. It was just a thought."

A laugh bubbled up from deep inside her. When the eruption had passed and she could talk again, she said, "The mistake you made was not taking me to your apartment? That's what you wanted to talk about?"

"Yeah, and that's funny because . . . ?"

"It's not funny. It's great. I'd love to spend the weekend with you." She picked up a slice of the bread from the platter and ate it in two bites. "I expected you to say . . . never mind. It doesn't matter."

"What? You expected me to say what?"

"It's not important. Really." She shrugged her shoulders, talking through a mouth full of bruschetta.

He reached over and brushed breadcrumbs from the side of her mouth. "It must have been important. I've seen suspects on a perp walk look happier than you did when you came in here. And you turned down bruschetta, which must be a first. Tell me what you expected."

She swallowed what she'd been chewing. "I thought . . . I was afraid you were going to say we made . . . you made . . . a big mistake going to bed with me last night and we should forget it happened."

"Jesus, sugar, I don't want to forget last night; I want to repeat it." His smile warmed every part of her he'd kissed the night before. "Is that the reason you wouldn't come to dinner at my place? You thought I was softening you up so I could dump you?"

"Well, let me down gently, was what I thought. But yes, that's the general idea."

"I'll be damned. I thought you wanted to meet in public because you were going to give me hell and wanted people around so I wouldn't lose my temper. But when you walked in you looked unhappy, not angry, I couldn't figure it out."

"Why would I want to give you hell?"

"I don't know. Standing you up for breakfast? Not nailing down our dinner? Leaving you in the middle of the night? Being bad in bed?"

"Bad in bed? That's the last reason . . . Didn't I say last night that you were good at . . . ?" She could feel her face flush and stopped talking when she saw his grin, this time more sexy than sweet.

"Oh, I remember what you said. I just wanted to hear it again." He finished his Scotch. "Drink up, I have a dinner waiting." He took her hand. "We back on solid ground here, Keyes? No more sad-puppy eyes because you're sure I'm about to—what was it you said—let you down gently?"

"Yeah, we're okay. Thanks. Or I'm sorry. Maybe both."

He kissed the inside of her wrist. "I love the perfume you wear. What's it called?"

She untangled her hand from his, picked up her glass and drained the last of the Scotch from it. "It's one of those embarrassing names."

"If it's 'Seduce Me Tonight,' I'd be happy to oblige."

She couldn't tell if he was flirting or making fun of her. "It's something like that, yes." After a brief hesitation, she replied, "It's called 'Beautiful'."

"A man gave it to you, I bet. And he was right. You are."

Tony's apartment was in a high rise a few blocks from the Bellevue. After they discreetly checked her out of the hotel, they moved her rental car to his parking garage.

He led her to his apartment on the fifteenth floor and opened the door to a living room with dove gray walls and blonde hardwood floors. Minimal furnishings with a masculine style graced the living room: a black leather modular couch on two walls with a low glass table in front of it. In the dining area, a small table on a white and black area rug with two chairs.

She was immediately drawn to the far side of the room where a sliding glass door opened onto a balcony that stretched across the entire length of the apartment's outside wall with a tiny bit of the statue of Billy Penn on top of City Hall visible from one corner. Coming back into the room she said, "This is wonderful. It feels, I don't know, serene, peaceful, almost Zen-like."

"That's what Mary Ellen said I needed."

"I forgot, she's an interior designer, isn't she? She did a great job."

"I'll tell her you liked it." Gesturing toward a short hallway, he said, "Here, I'll give you the thirty-second tour of the rest."

He pointed out a half-bath and a small room furnished with a desk, computer and file cabinet as well as a weight machine. Then he took her suitcase into his bedroom and put it on an armless rocking chair Margo remembered from his mother's house. A king-size bed with a half dozen pillows and a comforter with thin stripes in shades of gray, black and white and a long double dresser half-covered in family photos with a mirror over it were the only other pieces of furniture in the room.

With her back to him, she opened her bag and tried to decide what she should do next. It's not like she had a ton of experience spending weekends in men's apartments. Did you unpack? Wait for instructions? What? She picked up her toiletries bag, feeling awkward.

He seemed to read her thoughts. "Why don't you put that in the bathroom? You can share with me or you can have the little one to yourself, although the only shower's in here."

"Sharing's fine, thanks."

In the master bath, she saw that he had not only cleared space on the vanity for her but had put out an extra glass and clean towels. That and the smell of clean linen in the bedroom, as if he'd changed the sheets, too, calmed her.

Before she could decide what to do next, he took her in his arms saying, "You've been a major distraction today. I kept looking at my watch, wanting the day to be over so I could see you, hoping I had a chance to do this again." The kiss went from zero-to-sixty in two seconds flat, picking up where they left off the night before as though it was only minutes ago. It took her breath away and turned her insides all soft and wet.

"You were pretty distracting today, too," she said when she could breathe again.

"Good distracting like this," he said as he surfed his hands down her back, moving her close against him and covering her neck with kisses. "Or bad distracting like worried I was about to ditch you."

"Some of both. Well, maybe mostly the latter. I thought maybe you'd say it would be better to go back to the way we were before."

He drew her hands up onto his shoulders. "There's no going back, sugar."

She started to kiss him again then stopped. "Why do you call me that? I mean, I love it but it's so Southern and South Philly hardly counts as Southern."

He gently kissed her lips. "You've always tasted sweet when I kissed you. I thought it was some kind of lip-stuff you wore until last night." He began to unbuckle her belt. "Now I know you taste sweet everyplace."

She smiled at him, knowing in advance the answer to the question she was about to ask. "What exactly are you doing, Tony?"

Dropping the belt on the bed, he unzipped her linen pants. "It's hot in here. Don't you think you have too many clothes on?"

Chapter 8

A while later, he came out of the bathroom dressed only in a pair of cutoff jeans that rode on his hips and cupped his butt almost as closely as she had recently done with her hands. She was in a T-shirt and bikini panties hanging up her suit.

As he walked past, she waylaid him with a smile. "This guy I used to go down the shore with wore cutoffs like that. I always thought he was trying to show off his body."

"Maybe he thought it would put the idea in your head to show off yours."

"I was in a bikini. What more could he want?"

He fake-leered at her. "By now you've figured it out, I assume."

She combed her fingers through the cloud of dark fur on his chest and down the line of hair to his navel, which she tickled before hooking her fingers under the waistband of his cutoffs.

Dropping a kiss on her head, he took both her hands in his. "If you want dinner you better not go any further. You're distracting me. Seriously."

She squinted at him, as if thinking hard. "And it smells wonderful, like I remember your mother's kitchen smelled. But you offer me a difficult choice. Do I want to eat pasta cooked by a good Italian cook or do I want to distract a hunky guy. I can't decide. I want both."

"You can have both, but first I think I should feed you. You get cranky when you're hungry. And is that how you describe me to your friends? A hunky guy?"

"No, I say you're an old friend."

"I like hunky guy better."

"I'll think about it. Although all they'd have to do is see you like this and words wouldn't be necessary."

He looked behind her, diverted by something. "You don't wear this under those lawyer suits of yours, do you?" He reached around and came back with a black lace demi-bra dangling from one finger.

She snatched it back from him. "Yes, sometimes."

"Jesus, I'm sorry I know that. If I was ever a witness for you in court, I wouldn't be able to get my testimony straight thinking about what you had on underneath your jacket."

"No one in their right mind would let me prosecute a case you were involved in, detective. Not after this weekend. I think you're safe."

"Thank God." He pulled on a T-shirt and started for the kitchen. "Ten minutes to dinner. You might want to put some clothes on." And he disappeared from the bedroom.

After she donned jeans, she followed and was assigned the job of finding music to accompany their meal. She perused his CD collection finding the Springsteen, U2 and Italian opera she expected and some of the same jazz she had, but it was Andrea Bocelli she put on. He approved, but took the fifth when she asked if it was the music he used to seduce women.

After a dinner of pasta with his mother's marinara sauce, a tossed salad and bread, they moved to the couch. They sat for several hours finishing up a bottle of Chianti Classico talking comfortably, like Tony and Margo, the friends of a thousand years, not awkwardly like lovers of only one day.

Until he said, "Okay, there's something else I need to say to you," and she felt tension return to her shoulders. He must have seen it because he said, "It's nothing bad. It's more like a confession."

"Doesn't that require a priest?"

"If I started with a priest tonight, I might still be with him the next time you came back to Philly. No, this is something I have to confess to you." He took a sip of wine. "It . . . ah . . . wasn't your mom's idea to sign you up for the reunion. It was mine."

"Yours? Why?"

"Mary Ellen's wedding reception. Our unfinished business."

She looked down into the wine glass. "I half expected you to call or email me after that."

"When I went back to the room and you weren't there, I figured you'd changed your mind. I wasn't sure you wanted to hear from me. I decided I'd start over the next time you were in town, maybe cook dinner for you, like tonight. But I was in D.C. when you were here in April. Then the announcement about the reunion arrived. I told Dolores about it and she said . . . "

"She always wants me to do something other than take care of things for her when I come to Philly but I never do."

"Heard that before, have you? Anyway, she signed you up. Told me when you'd be at her house and suggested I 'accidently' run into you and ask you to go with me."

"So you ran a con on me with my mother's help? Or was it vice versa?"

"I'm not really sure. Whatever her plan was, mine was to get you here after the reunion dinner, which was where I was headed before my nephew interrupted us at the reception."

"But we were slow dancing at the reception—well, before you danced me down the hall to that little dark room. And you didn't want to slow dance at the reunion."

"Do you remember what song we were dancing to at the wedding?"

"No, do you?"

"It was 'I Can't Help Falling In Love With You' and I'd asked the DJ to play it at the reunion. But the plan sort of went south because you wouldn't wait until the right song was playing."

"I can't believe you remembered something like that." She reached over and touched his hand. "But I'd say the pager going off was more to blame for the plan blowing up than my insisting we dance to the wrong song."

He laced his fingers through hers. "Yeah, the damn pager even fucked up Plan B."

"Plan B?"

"Sunday. My goddamn pager goes off when I'm in the middle of kissing an almost-naked woman thinking my luck was holding."

"So last night was Plan C. I thought maybe it was because we were both, you know, happy about how well the presentation had gone. Or that we'd had too much to drink."

"I very carefully had only two drinks before we got to your hotel, which is hardly too much alcohol. And I'm not in the habit of bedding the nearest beautiful woman when I've had a good day."

"Not that you couldn't if you wanted to."

"What's that mean?"

"Beth said that you were . . . " She pulled her hand away and covered her mouth. "Oh, God, never mind. I think I've had too much wine tonight. Go back to what you were saying."

"No, I'm finished with my confession. Sounds like you have one to make, too." He settled back into the couch and half-smiled. "What'd Beth say?"

"Do I have to?"

He nodded.

She sighed. "All right. She said you were a person of interest, I guess would be a good description, with the women in the DA's office and the police department." She was twirling her wine glass by the stem, not looking him in the eye.

"And . . . ?"

"She said something about a virus."

That made him sit bolt upright. "Oh, for chrissake, she didn't tell you about that."

"You know about the Alessandro virus?"

"Yeah, a couple guys I work with found out about it and made sure they told me. In front of a whole lot of other guys I work with. It was fun." His expression said otherwise.

"She told me I looked like I had a bad case of it. Said I looked at you like you were dessert. I told her we were old friends but I don't think she believed me. Neither did Danny, for that matter."

"We are old friends. Now, we're more than that. Is that bad?"

"No, Tony. It's good."

He stood up and held out his hand. "So, now that we've both gotten our confessions out of the way, I'm ready to be distracted. How about dessert?"

"I think I'll pass, if you don't mind. I ate too much pasta."

He raised an eyebrow. "I thought Beth said you looked at me . . . "

"Oh, *that* kind of dessert."

*

Somewhere in the middle of the night she woke, unsure where she was for a few minutes until she saw Tony sleeping next to her. She tried to go back to sleep but she couldn't get her mind to turn off. It was like having a head full of possessed hamsters running around on squeaky wheels, pestering her with questions.

She eased her way out of bed, grabbed the first piece of clothing she found and went out to the darkened living room wearing Tony's T-shirt. She flicked on a small lamp and looked for something to read that might quiet the damned hamsters. But nothing among his criminal justice textbooks, sports biographies and paperback thrillers looked interesting enough to divert the little devils.

The view from the balcony caught her attention. She turned out the lamp and stood at the sliding glass door mesmerized by the lights of the city and lost in thought until she felt him slide his arms around her waist and nuzzle her neck.

"Here you are. You okay?"

She leaned back against his bare chest. "I'm fine, but I woke up and the hamsters in my head won't quiet down so I came out here.

The city looks beautiful at night, doesn't it?"

"Yeah, assuming you can forget there are dozens and dozens of burglaries, assaults, domestic violence incidents, drive-by shootings and who knows how many murders going on."

"You're killing the romance, Alessandro."

"And you and your hamsters aren't out here doing the same?"

"I wasn't thinking about murder and domestic violence, no."

"But if I know you—and I do—you're running those hamsters around trying to figure out something like what happens when we're old enough for Social Security—if there still is Social Security—and have to live on our pensions and support our aged mothers while we finish sending the last kid to graduate school."

"I'm not sure I love it or hate it that you know me that well."

"I love it that I do. Does that count?"

She turned and faced him, putting her hands on his chest. "I know I love . . . I've loved being with you this week."

He held her close. "Me, too. And, Margo, I don't know any more than you do what this means for next week or thirty years from now. I do know we can't figure it out tonight. I'm willing to take a chance we can in time. Are you?"

"I've never been very good at being here and now, Tony, or taking those kinds of risks. But for you, I'll try."

He kissed her gently. "Maybe there's a way I can get you here and now for a while, anyway. Want me to give it a try?"

Chapter 9

After breakfast on Saturday morning, Tony left for work saying he'd be back in a couple hours but would call to check in. Margo, the designated cook for that night, was about to leave for the Reading Terminal Market when the apartment phone rang. She answered on the second ring. "Hey, you. Miss me?"

There was silence from the other end.

"Hello?" she said.

A woman's voice said, "I'm sorry. I must have gotten the wrong number. I'm trying to reach Tony Alessandro." The caller sounded familiar, but Margo couldn't quite place her.

"You have the right number but he's not here at the moment. Can I take a message?"

"Just tell him his sister Catherine called."

"Oh, Catherine, hi. It's Margo Keyes."

"Margo? What are you . . . ? Never mind, none of my business. I'll call him on his cell. I assume he has it with him."

"I'm sure he does, it's not on his dresser. He's at work."

"I'll call him there." Catherine paused for a moment. "Will I get a chance to see you before you go back to the West Coast?"

"Probably not. I leave tomorrow. Maybe when I come back to see Mom in the fall?"

Twenty minutes later, as she was walking down Chestnut Street, her cell phone rang. This time she looked to see who it was, although the caller was no surprise. She'd been expecting this call.

"I'm sorry," she said when she picked up. "I'm really, really sorry."

"So you do know about caller ID," Tony said, laughing.

"Of course I do. I didn't look because I figured it was you."

"In the last twenty minutes I have heard from Catherine twice and once each from Theresa, Mary Ellen and Mom. It may be a record for all three sisters and my mom calling that close together."

"Oh, God, now I'm more than sorry. I'm scared."

"You should be. The second call from Catherine was to confirm the time for dinner at my mom's tonight with the full cast of my family plus your mother. We are to bring wine."

"Shit."

"Exactly. I wanted you to myself. Now I have to share."

"I don't know how else to say I'm sorry. At least I can get the wine." She laughed nervously. "Are you mad?"

"You mean, do I think you're a bad girl? No. Besides, I kinda like bad girls."

*

As she drove her rental car to the old neighborhood that evening, Margo asked, "Do you have any idea why this meeting of the clan has been called?" She tried to sound off-hand about it, although she was anything but.

He shook his head. "My sisters said they just wanted to see us. Although I did get a lot of questions about our going to the reunion together and what they seem to assume is a week of you staying with me."

"Damn it, I should never have left the hotel. All I'd have to deal with then was Greer if she saw you coming in and out of my room."

"I think it'll be okay tonight." He glanced over at her, his mouth twitching with amusement. "Although, now that I think about it, my sisters haven't seen much of you since you graduated from law school. So maybe they'll look at this as their chance to catch up on your religious habits, professional prospects, relationship status, that sort of thing. Don't think anyone will bother asking if you're still a virgin, not after a week of living with me." The amusement turned into a huge grin.

"Thanks, Alessandro, I was hoping for something a bit more comforting from you."

Margo pulled up to the curb at his mother's house a few minutes later. An uneasy feeling crept up the back of her neck as she got out of the car, as if she were being watched. She asked Tony if he felt it, too. He laughed.

"Of course, we're being watched. There are a dozen people inside, staring out every window. In fact . . . " He took her in his arms, backed her against the car and kissed her with enthusiasm.

She broke up the kiss by laughing. "What are you doing?"

"Giving them something to look at." He gave her a quick peck on the cheek, reached in the back seat of the car and brought out the bottles of wine they'd brought. Margo picked up the flowers she'd added to the wine purchases.

"Ready for this?" With his free hand, he took hers and they started up the path to the house. Before they got to the door, it opened and Theresa and Mary Ellen, the sisters on either side of Tony in age, came down the steps to greet Margo, while Catherine, the oldest of the four Alessandro siblings, stood in the doorway. They pulled her into the house leaving their brother to bring up the rear with the wine and the flowers he'd rescued from Margo when his siblings had captured her.

"Hey," he said, "what am I, chopped liver?"

"Tone, we see you all the time. We only see Margo at weddings," Theresa said. "Deal with it."

Two of the Alessandro daughters had been Margo's childhood playmates—ringleader Catherine, two years older than Margo and Tony, and best friend Theresa, less than a year older than the couple. Tag-along Mary Ellen, three years younger and the baby, had been the one they pulled in wagons, dressed in odd costumes and excluded from teenage conversations when they got to that stage. In the years since she'd moved to Portland, Margo had seen them mostly at their weddings or in passing when she visited her mother.

"Get Margo a glass of wine, Tony," Catherine ordered when they were all in the house. He gave a palms-up gesture of acquiescence and walked into the kitchen with the flowers and wine to obey Catherine's command.

Margo didn't see him again for almost an hour, trapped in the living room "catching up" with his sisters and an occasional husband or kid, a process that felt more like a job interview than a social conversation. When the interrogation sessions tapered off, Tony ambled in and perched on the arm of her chair, offering her wine from his glass as hers was now empty.

"How you holding up?" he asked. He took a sip of wine from the glass she'd handed back to him.

"The bar exam was easier. My last g-y-n appointment was more fun."

He almost choked on the wine. "Didn't you use to say you envied me having all these sisters?"

"I think I seriously over-romanticized the appeal."

"You're doing fine, sugar." He tipped up her chin, bent his head and kissed her.

"Is my brother annoying you?" Catherine said, from the door of the dining room.

Margo shook her head. "Actually, he stopped being annoying when we were about eleven or twelve. But in high school, when I wanted him to bother me, he didn't pay any attention." She looked up at him and smiled.

"We tried to teach him better but I guess we weren't successful," Catherine said with a grin that looked exactly like her brother's.

"I'm outta here," Tony said as he rolled off the arm of the chair. "If I learned anything from growing up with three sisters, it's that I can hold my own in this kind of conversation with one woman, but I'm in over my head with any more than that."

Catherine settled herself on the couch. "How are you doing, my dear? We can be a bit overwhelming, can't we?"

"I'm fine, Catherine. You know I've always loved your family. Don't you remember when I was maybe nine or ten and I tried to convince Tony he should swap places with me? I think I told him since he was the only boy he'd be happier being the only child and I'd be happier with all his sisters. I don't remember why I thought no one would notice the change, but I was convinced I could pull it off."

"There's another way to join the family, one I imagine my brother has thought of."

Celeste Alessandro came in just as Margo was trying to figure out how to respond, telling her oldest daughter, "You've all had Margo trapped in here since she arrived. Let her visit with her mother and get something to eat, please."

Margo escaped Catherine's scrutiny as fast as she could, walking toward the kitchen with her arm around Tony's mother.

"I want to thank you, Margo," Celeste said, patting Margo's hand.

"For what, Celeste?"

"For how my Anthony looks. He hasn't been this happy in a long time. It does my heart good to see him like this. You've put that beautiful smile back on his face and I'm grateful."

This wasn't quite the rescue Margo had thought it would be and she didn't know how to respond so she just patted Celeste's hand.

After filling her plate, Margo went into the back yard to find her mother enjoying the attention of some of the Alessandro grandchildren. She dropped to the ground next to Dolores' chair.

"You look distracted, Margo. Is something wrong?" Dolores asked, stroking her daughter's hair.

"Not wrong, exactly. I guess I'm uncomfortable about all this interest in Tony and me. It's not that big a deal, just old friends hanging out for a few days."

"Staying in his apartment is old friends hanging out? Well, if you say so." She patted her daughter's cheek.

"Mom, it's not like . . . " Margo stopped because it was exactly like that.

"Besides," Dolores continued, "you both look so happy. And it's no secret Celeste and I have always hoped that you two would get together."

Tony appeared at the top of the steps to the kitchen and motioned to her. He looked less relaxed than he had a few minutes before.

She followed him into the dining room, where no one was at the moment.

He took her hands. "I got paged."

"Oh, well," she began. "I'll wait for you . . . "

"I have to go to Newark," he interrupted.

"What's in Jersey?"

"Jameson's briefcase. Along with one dead and two live Russian mob guys, the Newark PD, and FBI agents not connected with the task force I'm working with, but who've apparently been trailing the Russians for months but have only now gotten around to letting us know about it." He ran his fingers through his hair. "So, it's officially fucked up beyond all recognition. One of my sisters can drive me home or I can call for a cab."

"No, I'll drive you. When will you be back?"

"Not sure. Probably not until after your flight leaves tomorrow. But you can stay at my place if you want."

"God, no. I don't want to be there without you. I'll take you home and come back here."

"This isn't how I planned to spend the rest of the weekend." He folded his arms around her and kissed her forehead.

She snuggled against his shoulder. "Me neither, but it's the way it works."

Tony said good-bye to his family and Margo made arrangements to return and stay with her mother. When they got to Tony's apartment, they packed their respective bags. Waiting in the lobby of his building for his ride, he put his arm around her. "If I say we need to talk, will you panic again?"

She laughed. "No, we do but I guess we'll have to do it on the phone."

"Unless . . . when will I see you again?"

"I wasn't planning to come back to Philly until September."

"Could you come back sooner? Or we could meet someplace— Chicago's about half-way."

"I'll talk to Jeff on Monday about a long weekend, maybe next month."

Before they could make any more plans, his ride arrived.

By the time Margo got back to Fir Street, the evening had progressed to dessert and after-dinner coffee. Theresa poured her a big glass of wine as soon as she walked in and led her to the couch in the living room where they could have some privacy.

"You okay?" she asked.

"I'm fine. This is what Tony does. Not much you can do about it."

"I was thinking more about what's going on between you two."

"Oh, that."

"Yeah, that. You and Tony."

"Me and Tony." Margo sighed. "I don't know what to say, Theresa. I'm still trying to figure it out."

"You want to hear my theory?"

"I might as well say yes. You'll tell me anyway."

"I think the two of you have been in love with each other since you were about fourteen. It's been there so long it's like background noise. You don't even notice it. It's way past time you did."

"You haven't told your brother this, have you?"

"Of course I have."

"What did he say?"

"Ask him." Theresa took Margo's hand. "I will say this. Today he was more like the Tony we all love than he's been in a long time. The grin on his face, that kiss outside . . ."

"Yeah, that was classic, wasn't it?" Margo smiled thinking about it.

"Except he hasn't been the Tony who'd do something like that in a long time. Mom says he's been happier this week than he's been in ages. So, I want to ask you a favor. As a friend."

"Anything. You've always been a good friend."

"Margo, I know you. You'll think of all the ways this won't work and then make sure one of them happens just to prove you're right. Or to keep from being hurt. Whatever. For once, don't do that. Just let it happen. You might be surprised how well it'll turn out."

Chapter 10

A plane flight had always been a way to get from one place to another while she napped. However, this time the trip home to Portland suspended Margo in thin air figuratively as well as literally, as she turned over and over in her mind what had happened in Philly.

Her life in Portland was predictable, under control, the way she liked things. What had happened with Tony was about as unpredictable as it got. There were a dozen reasons she could come up with for why it wasn't going to work, even more potentially bad consequences. But as soon as she started going down that road she heard Theresa's voice asking her not to.

Nothing about the situation sorted out into nice, neat boxes.

When the pilot announced their descent into the Portland airport she looked out the window for a sight she knew would comfort her—the Columbia River, gushing its way from a glacier in Canada to the Pacific. Seeing it always meant she was home.

But, in the end, the comfort of being home was superseded by discovering she had someone else's messenger bag. As soon as she discovered the error, she called the airline. The only good thing about it was she'd stuffed the bag so full of research materials she'd had to carry a purse, too, or she would have lost keys, wallet and credit cards along with her case files and iPod.

After she unpacked, she called Tony.

"Hey, sugar. How was your flight?"

"Tedious. Flight got canceled out of Seattle so I had a longer layover than I expected. And I got home with the wrong messenger bag. So, not great. How was Newark?"

"About the same as your trip," he replied. "We now have one less mobster to watch. The dead guy's been on our list for a while. He was killed with a weapon similar to the one that did Jameson so he's not the shooter Isaiah's looking for. And there wasn't a damn thing in Jameson's briefcase that looks like something worth killing over. Last, the two live Russians we picked up swear they don't know anything about anything."

"So what's this all about?"

"Deal gone bad, probably, although we don't have hard evidence. We think Jameson may have been trying to sell Microsoft information to someone. Problem with that theory is, Microsoft says there was nothing in the briefcase worth selling. And it doesn't explain how we ended up with two bodies."

"What do our federal friends say?"

"Not much. The ones I'm working with are as baffled as I am. The new kids on the block have been tailing the Russians—the same Russians who were found with the body—for weeks and didn't see them shoot anyone. So they're not likely to be the bad guys. It could be the internal politics of a struggle for control of the Bratva. Haven't talked to our contacts in the Russian community yet. That'll happen tomorrow."

"So not exactly a cleared case."

"No, just more mud in the water." His voice changed to a softer tone. "Let's talk about something less frustrating. I hear you had a long talk with Theresa."

"Yeah."

When she didn't go further he said, "What'd you think about her theory?"

"She told me to ask you what you said when she told you."

"Ah. So I get to go first. Okay, I laughed it off as another of her interferences in my life. But after I thought about it for a while, it seemed possible. Now, I'm positive it's right."

"Me, too. But I don't know what that means."

"I don't either. We'll have to sort it out as we go along."

She sniffled, trying not to cry. "I've been trying to figure it out and . . ."

"We need time to figure it out together."

"That's hard to do when we live so far apart."

"We can have a weekend together every now and then. You'll be here in September. Maybe come to Philly for the holidays like your mother always wants. I have a lot of vacation time I haven't used. And I've never been to the West Coast. We can do it, if that's what we want." He paused. "If that's what *you* want."

"I think so. Do you?"

He said without any hesitation, "Absolutely. I want to give us a chance."

She was silent for a moment. "But, Tony, we have to be honest with each other."

"Haven't we always been?"

"Yes, at least up until now. There's something I need to tell you. First, is theft of soap a misdemeanor punishable in the state of Pennsylvania?"

"Theft of what? Soap? What are you talking about?"

"I wanted something to remind me of you so I took the soap from your bathroom."

When he stopped laughing, he said, "So, that's where it went. Jesus, sugar, if it turns out this is in the criminal code, you could be disbarred."

"I know. Will you promise not to turn me in if it's against the law?"

"I'll have to think about it. How about I call tomorrow night about seven your time? I'll let you know whether there's a warrant out on you for soap theft and you find out about a long weekend." He paused for a heartbeat or two. "I know we can make this work, Margo."

"Can we, Tony?"

*

Margo had been working for two hours clearing her desk and computer of what had accumulated while she was away when Kiki Long popped her head into the office. When Margo had left on her trip, the twenty-four-year old paralegal had shoulder-length, platinum-blonde hair with dark brown roots. Now what Margo could see of her hair over a bright orange 1940s Rosie the Riveter head wrap, was brown with a big pompadour in the front. She wore lipstick to match the head wrap and had replaced last month's black leggings, ballet tee and mesh sweater with men's pleated front trousers and a vintage Hawaiian sport shirt.

What hadn't changed—what couldn't change—were the climbing rose tattoos that twined around her arms, hid shyly under her shirtsleeves to burst out around her neck in red blossoms.

"Welcome back, Margo. I missed you. How was Philadelphia?"

"It was great, thanks. What happened around here while I was gone that's worth knowing about?"

"Not much. Willow, the jury clerk, is finally pregnant. Vince the security guard and his partner, Charlie, broke up after twenty years. That's about it." Kiki cocked her head and frowned slightly. "But something happened with you. You look different." She circled the desk, studying her friend. "A bright blue shirt? No jacket? Who knew you even owned clothes like that?"

"Kiki, I have work to do and so . . ."

"Something happened . . . like . . . oh, my God . . . of course . . . you had sex with the guy from the plane. Was he just a hook-up? Will you see him again? Was he incredibly handsome? He must have been very, very sexy to get you to look all glow-y like this."

"Stop. There was no man from the plane. I just had a good vacation. End of story." From the sudden, extreme heat and flushing she could feel, all the blood in her body had taken up residence in her face.

"You're blushing worse than I've ever seen. There's something going on." Kiki walked out the door, saying, "I'll find out. You know I have ways."

Margo went back to the pile on her desk. Buried in her caseload, she forgot about Kiki's curiosity so when the younger woman walked into her office several hours later with a latte in her hand, Margo didn't think anything of it. She should have known better. Kiki didn't get lattes for anyone unless she thought there was a payoff, usually in the form of information.

Kiki put the cup down in front of Margo. "Here's what I found out: off and on during the week in Philly you were seen with a drop-dead gorgeous guy. He's about six feet tall, has the sexiest brown eyes on the Eastern seaboard and a body to die for. He's a police detective. You graduated from high school with him. You looked especially cozy in the bar at your hotel after the big dinner and the next night, too. I'm guessing he's who put that look on your face." She cocked her head and smirked.

"For God's sake, Kiki, who've you been talking to? I was at a conference, not having a wild week. The guy I was with was my co-presenter. We were planning our presentation and enjoying our success." Margo pushed the cup back toward Kiki. "Here, give this to someone else. No latte is worth this cross-examination."

"Keep it. I know I'm right. You're blushing again. I always protect my sources but I will say, my source says Danny was pretty envious of you and Greer thought . . ."

"Danny Hartmann told you? And Greer's talking? Jesus."

"No, I didn't hear it from Danny. She just mentioned something about it to someone at the Justice Center who told someone over here who told me. And you know Greer. She always talks about the good-looking men she meets. If he made it onto her radar, he must be a stunner. When will he be here so we can meet him?"

"Never, if I can help it. It's my private life. Leave it."

With a parting smirk, Kiki opened the door only to bang into

Jeff Wyatt, the Multnomah County District Attorney, her boss, as well as everyone else's. She apologized and scampered back to her desk.

"What was all that about?" Jeff asked. He scrutinized Margo's face. "Whatever it was, you're blushing."

"Just Kiki's usual gossip-mongering. I swear, she could work on one of those TV entertainment shows, she's that good."

"I'm just grateful she's on my side. It'd scare the devil out of me if she was on the wrong side of the law."

"Point well taken. You have something for me, boss?"

"Eventually, but first I wanted to thank you for standing in for me at the conference. I heard great things about your presentation. It was the hit of the day, a colleague from Seattle said."

"Really? I thought we did better than just hit of the day."

"Okay, maybe he did say it was one of the best presentations he heard. Actually, he asked if you'd repeat it at the West Coast DA's meeting next year."

"Happy to. Just me or does this get my co-presenter a free ticket to the West Coast?"

"I hear you know the guy you presented with."

"We grew up together. Been friends for years."

"Just friends?"

Margo knew better than to try and fool her boss. Wyatt looked like the man half the witnesses to a crime described—medium height, medium build, medium coloring, no visible scars or outstanding features. But behind the average Joe looks was the best legal mind in the state and one of the savviest observers of his fellow humans anywhere.

"We've dated, yes. But not . . . " She stopped. But not what? Recently? Lie. Seriously? Also a lie.

"Not so you want to talk about it, apparently."

"Thanks. That's about it."

"Well, good luck with it. If that's what Kiki has her teeth

into, you're doomed." He started back to his office. "When you have time this afternoon, I do have a couple new cases I'd like you to look at."

She indicated the mess on her desk. "Oh, sure, Jeff, because I don't have anything else to do."

"Like I said, Margo, welcome back."

*

"Margo, Sam Richardson. You lose a briefcase?" The phone call from across the park at Central Precinct came first thing after Margo got to work two days later.

"Has the city run out of bad guys for you to chase? Or has Chris Angel decided you're best suited to running some bureaucratic boondoggle like the lost and found?" She considered Sam Richardson one of the best homicide detectives in the Portland Police Bureau and he returned her admiration. But as much as she respected him—and loved his wife, a well-known glass artist—giving him a hard time was still part of their relationship.

"My boss wouldn't put me in charge of anything that challenging so I continue to serve and protect. That doesn't usually include missing luggage. However, this morning inside a messenger bag under a body in Forest Park, I found business cards with the DA's logo on them and the name Margo Keyes. Good detective that I am, it led me to believe that the bag might belong to someone with that name in Jeff's office. Want to clear my case for me and confess to the deed? Or, would you rather get back to my original question and tell me if you lost your briefcase?"

"Ugh. Not exactly how I wanted my stuff found. But found is good. I guess. I didn't lose it. It got swapped with someone else's on the Seattle leg of my flight home last Sunday. The one I turned in to Alaska Airlines belonged to Brandy Nixon. Is that your vic's name?"

"That's her. And she had a boarding pass for an Alaska flight from Sea-Tac to PDX in her purse so that clinches it. Listen, since you live out by the airport, any chance you can get hers back and save me a trip out there? I'll call and tell them to expect you."

"I'll see what I can do. If I get it, I'll bring it to you tomorrow. I'm in court most of the day so it'll be late afternoon."

"No hurry. The owner doesn't need it where she is."

Chapter 11

"It took you longer than I expected to find your way across the park." Danny Hartmann greeted Margo as she got off the elevator at Central Precinct.

"Hello to you, too, Danny. Although I don't know why I should be pleasant to you. Thanks to you, Kiki's on my case about Tony. At least he's three thousand miles away and out of her reach."

"What the fuck are you talking about? I didn't say anything to Kiki. And what do you mean he's three thousand miles away?" The detective looked confused.

Margo scanned the area looking for Sam. "Your partner around? I told him I'd be over after I got out of court. I need to . . . "

"What's Sam got to do with your being here?"

Now it was Margo's turn to be confused. "Are we in the same conversation? I'm here about the dead woman in Forest Park, the one who had my messenger bag. What're you talking about?"

Danny looked over Margo's shoulder. "I think it's all about to get straightened out."

From behind her, Margo heard the distinctive sound of Sam's cowboy boots on the hard floor. "There he is. Sam, I . . . "

But it wasn't Sam who said, "What's a nice girl like you doing in a place like this?" Nor was it Sam who put a possessive hand on the small of her back. And it sure as hell wasn't his cologne she smelled.

"Tony?" When she saw both Sam Richardson and Tony, her eyes widened and she could feel her face pale as she struggled to get words out. "You're here? How'd you . . . ? When . . . ?"

Danny rolled her eyes heavenward. "Hallelujah. I have lived to see the miracle of a speechless lawyer."

Margo looked back and forth between the two men standing in front of her, grins on both their faces. They made an interesting contrast. Shorter by three or four inches and older by close to a decade, Sam's slightly sun-bleached, sandy-brown hair and weathered skin reflected his outdoor lifestyle as much as Tony's dark hair and olive skin showed his Mediterranean heritage. The Philly cop's taste in clothes ran to a well-tailored gray suit, white shirt and burgundy tie; the detective born in Eastern Oregon wore jeans with no tie and a blue shirt. And Tony's Italian loafers were half a world away from Sam's cowboy boots, a reminder he was raised on the ranch his great-grandfather had homesteaded.

What was almost identical was the stare. Two pairs of brown eyes were looking at Margo, Sam's full of amusement, Tony's affection, while she stood rooted to the floor, trying to find her composure, or at least her voice. Eventually she got out, "You didn't you tell me you were coming to Portland."

"I wanted it to be a surprise."

"Well, that worked out for you," she said.

Sam frowned. "Christ, Margo, you're the color of Tony's shirt." To the wearer of the white shirt he said, "Is this how East Coast men impress women? You scare the pea-wadding-green out of them so they have a heart attack?"

"It's how we weed out the weak ones," Tony said with a grin.

"What are you doing here?" Margo asked.

Sam said, "I work here, remember?"

"Not you, Sam." Margo said.

"Following the breadcrumbs from Newark." As Tony explained why he was there, she fought the urge to throw herself at him, to kiss him, to hold him. Finally, having heard——or at least, understood—little of what he said, she put up her hand.

"Slow down. I still don't understand. The Russians led you here?"

"Sort of. Mostly it's because the working group of local and federal agencies here is further along in investigating this string of intellectual property thefts. So, against all odds and previous experience, we're not going to reinvent the wheel but build on it. I flew in a couple hours ago with two feds. A guy from Long Beach and a woman from Seattle are due in soon."

"That's where Jeff is this afternoon, isn't it, Sam?" When Sam nodded, she added, "Jeff Wyatt's my boss, Tony."

"And they're all waiting for us," Sam said to his new colleague. "But ten minutes of doing penance for scaring her's okay. They'll keep for that long." He started to walk away.

"Sam, I'm here to see you," Margo said.

"To what do I owe that honor?"

"The messenger bag? From the woman in Forest Park?"

"Christ, apparently you're not the only one made witless by the arrival of our out-of-town guests. You get the bag back from the airline?"

"Right here." She handed him a dark charcoal gray leather bag. "I thought I was going to have to get a court order to retrieve it, but they finally gave it to me." She turned to Tony. "Remember I said I'd gotten home with the wrong messenger bag?" He nodded. "Well, Sam found it."

Sam snorted. "Not sure 'found' is the best description. A hiker stumbled on a body in a wilderness park in the West Hills where perps like to leave dead people they want to hide. The woman had Margo's briefcase with her."

"I apparently swapped bags with this woman who sat next to me on the flight from Seattle when we pulled them out of the overhead. Mine is exactly like this."

"Let's get this done, counselor, and then Tony can walk you out."

Fifteen minutes later, Margo and Tony were out on the sidewalk. "When exactly were you going to tell me you were in town?" she asked.

"Called you when we got in but it went to voice mail. So, I

was waiting until I had five minutes to myself to try again. Failing that, I figured I'd call tonight and make plans for the weekend."

"I was in court most of the day. That's why you got voice mail. And I must have forgotten to tell you I'd be home late tonight. Not to mention that I have plans for the weekend."

"Oh," he looked dejected. "Maybe the surprise thing wasn't such a good idea."

"We-e-el-l-l," she dragged out the word as if thinking seriously about her options, "I suppose I could change my weekend plans."

From the grin on his face, he wasn't taking the bait. "I wouldn't want you to disappoint some guy by making you change plans."

"The only guy who might be disappointed would be you if you didn't like the plans I changed to include you."

"What're we doing?"

"A hike in the Columbia River Gorge on Saturday, then dinner and a soak in the hot tub of a room at the Bonneville Hot Springs."

"Sounds like fun." He raised an eyebrow. "If I take you out for dinner tonight, could you find extra space in your room for me?"

"I'll think about it." She smiled. "As for dinner, I have no idea what's waiting for me when I get to my office. Probably won't be finished until seven. Then I promised I'd meet a friend at the First Thursday opening at a local gallery."

"We're likely to be in meetings until late, too. And Sam said something about going to First Thursday for his wife. Is she an artist?"

"She is. And the opening I'm going to is an exhibit of her work. So Sam'll get you out in time to go to the gallery. I'll leave your name with security at that door . . . " she pointed to the door on the east side of the courthouse. "The guard can direct you to my office."

"Sounds good." He drew her into his arms and kissed her, a long, tender, and promising kiss. "Been looking forward to that ever since I boarded the plane. See you later, sugar." He took the steps two at a time back into police headquarters.

She stood on the sidewalk for a few moments trying to sort out how her life had just changed.

A little before seven, Margo heard a commotion outside her office. It sounded like women giggling. In a few minutes, Kiki to come into her office, eyes wide. "Did you see that guy who came in with Jeff? He's McSteamy and McDreamy rolled into one."

Before Margo could go to the door and look, the object of everyone's attention appeared at her office door. She might have known.

"Ready to go, counselor?" Tony asked. "We're meeting Sam and his wife at the gallery."

"Give me five minutes." It was tempting to torture Kiki but she introduced them.

"Sweet. So, you're the guy." Kiki and Tony shook hands. "Alessandro's Italian, isn't it?" she asked. "Do you speak Italian?"

"It is and I do. At least enough to flirt with and read a menu," Tony said with an expression suited to the first use of his language skills.

"Say something in Italian."

"*Quella donna dietro lo scrittorio e molto bella.*"

"Which means . . . ?"

"That woman behind the desk is very . . . "

"Okay, Tony, enough with the language lessons," Margo said.

"I have to get out of here for my date, anyway," Kiki said. "Come back again and teach me some more, Tony." She wiggled her fingers goodbye, almost skipped out of the room, picked up her backpack and left for the day.

*

The Fairchild Gallery was in the Pearl District, Portland's newest upscale neighborhood where art galleries, trendy restaurants and high-rise condos shared space with an armory, now renovated into a theater, a high-end grocery and outdoors equipment stores. Liz Fairchild had relocated her gallery there from a smaller space in Northwest Portland about two years before. She'd never regretted the move. Especially not on evenings like tonight with crowds of people dropping by after work to see the show of Amanda St. Claire's new glass art pieces.

Liz, as always, was welcoming everyone in person, dressed tonight in an emerald green silk tunic over leggings that showed off her long, shapely legs. The streak in her brown hair and the polish on her well-manicured fingernails, as well as the color of her eyes, matched the tunic.

The place was crowded for the monthly opening. But only one of the people Liz was looking for had arrived. "Fiona," she said in her distinctive, I-used-to-smoke voice, "I'm glad you're here. Amanda is in her usual state of panic about no one she knows showing up. She'll be glad to see you. I think she was expecting Margo, too."

"You mean she isn't here already? We're supposed to meet her here and I thought we were late." Fiona McCarthy kissed the older woman's cheek and so did her date.

With mahogany red hair and creamy skin as well as a name like McCarthy it wasn't hard to figure out Fiona's ethnic heritage. A reporter for Portland's weekly alternative newspaper, *Willamette Week*, she was with Mark Howard, a reporter with the daily paper, *The Oregonian*. They'd been dating for over a year and most people who knew them assumed it was serious so suited for each other were they.

"If she's here, I have yet to see her and I'm pretty sure I've said hello to everyone, although it is crowded." Liz looked around the gallery again and, when she still didn't see Margo, shrugged her shoulders.

"Where's Amanda?" Fiona said. "I'll go give her some moral support until Margo gets here."

"I'm right here." The voice came from behind where a five-foot nothing little bit of a thing with caramel-brown curls and huge hazel eyes stood. Hard to guess from her looks that this was the artist in question. Amanda St. Claire looked more likely to be writing poetry in a garret than wrestling with tabletop-sized sheets of glass and twenty-pound kiln shelves. But everyone who knew art glass knew her as one of the most creative and talented artists in the region.

With her was her husband. Even for his wife's opening, Sam stuck to his cowboy boots and jeans, although as a concession to the evening, he had put on a jacket.

"And if you're looking for Margo, be patient. Sam says an out-of-town guest has just arrived so she may be a little late." Amanda looked up at her husband with a knowing smile.

"Out-of-town guest? Has her mother finally decided to come see her?" Fiona asked.

"Not exactly," Amanda said. "I hear . . . "

"Well, if that's her guest, I'm surprised she showed up at all," Liz interrupted. She was looking toward the front of the gallery where Margo and Tony were just walking in. "I sure as hell wouldn't be wasting my time at an art gallery if he came to visit me."

Tony had his arm around Margo's shoulders and she was looking up at him, laughing. His head was cocked to the side to get closer to her face as he spoke and the smile on his face went up into his brown eyes, lighting them up. She leaned into him, maybe to hear what he was saying, maybe just to be close to him.

"Holy shit. Who's that?" Fiona asked.

"A Philadelphia police detective. He's an old friend, she says. But they sure look like more than friends to me," Sam responded.

"We should all have old friends who look like that," Liz said. "He's gorgeous."

"Lotta women in the Justice Center share your opinion," Sam said. "We had a parade of them through our floor today with the most wild-ass excuses for being there. Some of them giggled like goddamn teenagers." He shook his head in disbelief.

"You said you'd been told he was a good cop, Sam. You didn't tell me he was to-die-for good-looking," Amanda said.

"Why would I notice something like that?" her husband said, his voice close to a growl.

The couple made it to the knot of Margo's friends. She apologized for being late and started to make introductions.

Liz cut her off. "Hello, handsome. I'm Liz. Where've you been hiding?" She clasped the hand he held out in both of hers and didn't let go.

Margo explained how she knew Tony and gave an abbreviated explanation of what he was doing working with the Portland police.

"Honey, what would it take for you to fly someplace to work with me? I'm willing to do anything up to and including murder." Liz actually batted her eyelashes at Tony. And kept holding his hand.

"Liz, I'm sure we wouldn't want you to neglect your other patrons," Margo said.

"They can wait. I'd like to get to know Tony a little better." She tucked his hand under her arm and led him away.

"Leave it to Liz to commandeer the new guy before the rest of us are even introduced," Amanda said. "But it means I don't have to worry she'll take off with Sam tonight."

"Yeah, I think he's safe. Tony's the target this time," Margo said, laughing.

Mark Howard said, "As long as we're talking about good-looking people, who's that blonde over there? She's the most beautiful woman in the room."

Margo wasn't sure if she was more annoyed her friend's date was describing another woman that way or if it was the woman in question.

"That's Greer Payne. I work with her. She's a deputy DA," Margo said.

"*That's* a DA? Wow. Who knew they looked like that?" Howard said.

Margo rolled her eyes. And when Amanda looked like she was about to comment, she shook her head to signal her to leave it. Fiona avoided their eyes as her boyfriend went slack-jawed watching Greer in a navy blue tailored suit which was both going-to-court appropriate and, somehow, sexy.

With her was Paul Dreier, a local attorney. Dressed in Armani, his light brown hair carefully styled without a strand out of place, and his manicured nails and expensive-looking shoes both buffed to a high-gloss shine, he was a perfect match for Greer. Paul and Greer. Ken and Barbie. The only difference, according to most people who knew them, was that Greer had more brains than Barbie and a better wardrobe.

Greer must have had her radar out because just as Tony returned, she led her date over to the group. After the introductions, Greer extended her hand to him, peeked up from under her thick, perfectly mascara-ed eyelashes and said, "I'm so glad to see you again. I didn't know we'd be seeing each other this soon."

"Nice to see you, too, Greer."

"Are you here on business or pleasure?"

"A little of both." He smiled at Margo, who changed the subject.

"Amanda, tell me about your new work," she said.

"It's a further exploration of combining glass with metals. This time I used both foils and wire. I'm really enjoying playing with it. And I've started using reactive glass that changes color when I incorporate metal so I get an extra kick."

"I love this piece," Margo said, indicating a gently curved rectangle of creamy vanilla glass with a wide stripe in the middle created by the reaction of the glass with the metal foils. "It would look great with the other piece of yours I have." She looked at the tag identifying the piece by name and price. "But you're moving out of my price range, Amanda. Good for you. Bad for me."

"That's why I married her," Sam said. "I couldn't afford to buy her work."

The group broke up into duos and trios; the conversations waxed and waned; various configurations of people went to look at what was on display or to refresh their glasses of wine. During one of the wanings of the group, Greer went off to get more wine, Tony went to the back, toward Liz's office and Paul Dreier sidled up to Margo as she perused the jewelry case. Standing behind her and in a low voice he said, "Margo, we have something we need to talk about. How about lunch tomorrow?"

She didn't turn to respond to him. "What would we have to talk about, Paul? You don't have any clients involved with our office."

"One of my clients—I'm not at liberty to disclose who—is concerned about a deal you've gotten involved in that could be dangerous. He asked me . . . "

"A deal? A plea deal? I've been on vacation. I haven't gotten into negotiations with anyone since I've been back. And even if I had, I wouldn't discuss it with you or your client."

"I think you should listen to his advice. What do you say, lunch tomorrow?"

She glanced around and waved to Tony before she responded. "I rarely have lunch out, Paul. But if you want an appointment, call the office and I'll see what we can set up."

Dreier gripped her elbow to keep her from leaving. "Margo, I'm serious. My client is very well informed and listening to what he has to say could save you a great deal of trouble."

Before she could respond, Tony rescued her. "Sorry to interrupt, but I'm hungry and jet-lagged."

Margo shook free of Paul's grip. "If you need to talk to me and can't make an appointment, just come into the office and if I'm free, I'd be happy to continue our conversation."

Before they left, Margo looked one more time at the piece of Amanda's work she'd fallen in love with, the piece that now had a red dot on the display tag, indicating it was sold. Tony got a kiss from Liz. Fiona extracted a promise from Margo to have lunch so they could "talk" and Greer gave Tony a particularly long handshake and said she'd look forward to seeing him again soon. Amanda couldn't leave the reception yet, so Tony and Margo were on their own for dinner.

Waiting for the light to change so they could cross the street, Tony said, "Tell me about Dreier. He's the only one I didn't get a chance to talk to."

"He's so . . . I don't know . . . snake-oil salesman, I guess. The kind of lawyer who gives lawyers a bad name. He represents business clients all up and down the West Coast, Seattle to LA with two or three things in common—shady business ethics, a lot of money, and overseas factories for most of them. I sure wouldn't want his practice. Although he does enjoy the perks—Armani suits, a huge penthouse condo somewhere around here, a new luxury car every year."

"Do you have to deal with him often?"

She slipped her arm through his as they crossed the street. "Hardly ever. He's retained to keep his clients out of trouble with us. But he hangs around the office a lot. I think he uses it as a place to pick up women."

"I take it you're not one of them."

"Good God, no. But, speaking of hitting on people, why did Liz take you off like that?"

"Asking questions about us. She didn't get too far. This big guy came in. White hair, but looks too young to have it. Colin maybe? Whoever he is, as soon as he walked in, he kissed her and she lost interest in me."

"Ah, you met Collins. He's a metal sculptor. Been one of Liz's artists since she opened her first gallery. They've had a relationship since then, too. They own a house together here but he has his studio in Eastern Oregon. Comes to town every couple of weeks. And, you're right, when they see each other, the rest of the world disappears. But once he leaves town, she'll be calling me and asking questions. Hell, first I had Beth, Danny and Greer asking questions, then Kiki, now Liz. You sure do stir up interest from my women friends, Alessandro."

Chapter 12

"You're quiet. Something wrong?" Finished with his hamburger and every single French fry he'd been served, even the tiny bits of overcooked ones, Tony glanced covetously across the table at what was left on Margo's plate. They'd had to wait for a table at the popular Deschutes Brewpub and during the wait she swore he'd moved from hungry to ravenous.

"It's noisy in here and I'm tired. It's been a long day." She pushed her plate with the half-eaten burger and fries across to him. "You must be tired, too. It's been an even longer day for you."

He cleaned up her leftover fries, then seemed to realize she was playing with her glass of beer as a way of avoiding his eyes. His head tilted, he frowned at her. "It's more than being tired. You're not happy about something. Is it because I'm here or because I didn't tell you I was coming to Portland? I could have told you last night on the phone. It just seemed fun to . . . anyway, I apologize if you didn't like being surprised."

"No, I loved the surprise. I'm glad to see you, really."

"Then what is it? Your body's here—which I'm enjoying looking at—but I don't have much of your attention. What's going on?"

"It's just that . . . oh, God, Tony, you know how I am." She looked up, directly at him. "Ever since I got back from Philly, I've been trying to make sense of what happened between us. But I haven't been able to. And now, before I can get it sorted out, here we are, all coupled up."

"Meaning . . . ?"

"Everyone thinks we're a couple. Our families. All my colleagues. Tonight all those people looking at us like . . . well, like 'Oh, aren't they a cute couple' . . . and Kiki and Liz making a fuss over us."

"And that bothers you because . . . ?"

"It doesn't bother me. It worries me. If it doesn't work out, will I make my mother unhappy, lose your sisters as my friends, piss off your mother, embarrass myself in front of everyone I work with, make my friends feel sorry for me because this gorgeous man dumped me?"

"Jesus, sugar, you worry about things that wouldn't even occur to anyone else. First of all, why do you think it won't work out between us?"

"I'm not saying that it won't. I'm just trying to anticipate what could happen. And even if it does work out, there's a whole other set of questions. Who's gonna move where? Will one of us end up with no job? Will I have to sell my house? Will your career be wrecked because that *Inquirer* reporter who knows every organized crime figure in Philly from Angelo Bruno on connects you with my father? How'll we deal with the long hours we both work?"

"I was wrong. That's beyond worrying. I don't even know what to call it. It must be hell inside that head of yours." He leaned across the table and took her hand. "No wonder you're so quiet. You're so busy coming up with all the things that can go wrong, you don't have any room left in your mind to think of a topic of conversation."

"It's not funny. It's . . . I don't know . . . it's . . . I can't figure it out."

"I'm not going to joke you out of this, am I? Okay, then I'll ask a serious question. Would you like to go away by yourself this weekend to work this out? I assume that's what the solitude in the wilderness is about."

"I was ready to go away and try to work it through but now that you're here, all I can think about is being with you."

"That's the best thing I've heard you say since I got here."

"Besides, didn't you say we should work this out together? A weekend away, just the two of us, would be a place to start, wouldn't it?"

"I'd vote for that. But are you sure that's what you want?"

"Yes, it'll be better being with you."

"Okay then, why don't we wait until we get back to Portland to tackle all those questions the hamsters are throwing at you?" he suggested. "How about one weekend of enjoying each other before we get too wrapped up in settling all the details of the next couple decades?"

"I think I can ignore my hamsters and their squeaky wheels and stupid questions for a weekend. As long as you can provide a diversion for me."

"Oh, I think I can manage that." He motioned to the waiter for the check. "And, just so you know, in answer to one of the questions, Theresa said if I fuck it up, not to bother coming home." He grinned at her. "She'd rather keep you in the family than me. She also said to remind you what you promised. She wouldn't tell me any more than that." He didn't have to ask the question, his expression did.

"She made me promise I wouldn't look for all the reasons this wouldn't work and make them happen, the way I usually do. She said to just let it unfold naturally. As you can tell, I'm struggling with it."

"Try it for the weekend, you might like it." He signed the credit card slip. "Can we get out of here? You're right. I'm beginning to feel the time difference and my four AM wake-up."

"Yeah, I imagine you are." She reached across the table, touched his hand. "Do you want to get your suitcase from the hotel where you've checked in and stay at my house instead?"

"I can't do that," he said, shaking his head.

"Oh, do you want me to stay with you?" He didn't answer. "Right, you said you were tired. You want to be by yourself tonight. I'll drop you off. Just tell me where."

"That won't work either."

"I don't understand."

He grinned. "I never checked into a hotel. We came straight from the airport to police headquarters."

"You've been waiting for me to ask you to stay with me, haven't you? And I've been slow at doing it."

"I was hoping you would ask. If you want to . . . "

"Where's your suitcase?"

"At Sam's desk."

"So the entire Portland Police Bureau knows, too."

"I didn't know you wanted to keep it under wraps. You should have told me." The grin and affectionate expression had been replaced by tensed shoulders and a thin-lipped mouth.

"No, no, no. I didn't mean it that way. I'm sorry. That was rude. You have every right to bite my head off."

He sat back in his chair, his body more relaxed now. "I'm not particularly interested in biting your head off. Nibbling your mouth, yes. Maybe your ears. Definitely your breasts."

"Tony!"

*

Twenty-five minutes after they left the city, Margo drove into a gated parking lot just off the levee along the Columbia River. After she parked, they went down the ramp to the dock and out to one of the smaller homes in the marina, a shake-covered two-story house with large cobalt blue pots of small evergreens and flowers flanking the door.

Once inside, she led him upstairs where she suggested he unpack.

As she moved some of her clothes around in the closet she said, "I have hangers here for your suit and I'll empty a drawer for you. Oh, and I have to get clean towels. There should be space on the vanity for your . . . "

"I'm not here to see your bathroom or inspect your clean

towels, Margo." He came behind her and put his hands on her waist, turning her around.

"I know. You're here to work, but you were . . . "

"No, work got me here but I'm here to see you. We started something when you were in Philly and I don't want it to slip away." He kissed her, a Tony kiss, hot, arousing, breathtaking.

"We better get to bed," she said. "We both have work tomorrow."

"Bed's good." His grin didn't look like he was thinking much about work.

"Speaking of work . . . "

"Were we?"

"I was. How'd you get this assignment, anyway?"

"Fought for it. There was some logic to it—I've been working with the task force for a while and had more than a nodding acquaintance with the Jameson case. Told the captain I had connections out here that would be valuable in the investigation."

"You have a lot on the line, then."

"Not really. My career, my personal life and maybe national security. Nothing important."

"Do you ever take anything seriously?"

"Yes. This." He kissed her again. "That's about as serious as I want to get right now. What was that about bed?"

"I have to go downstairs and turn the lights out and make sure everything's locked up. Before I do, can I hang up your suit for you so it doesn't get wrinkled?"

"That's not the sexiest invitation I've ever had to take my clothes off but, yeah, you can."

Chapter 13

When she woke at her usual 6 A.M., Margo found herself spooned against Tony's back and legs, her arm around him, the sheet barely covering them from their waists down. His chest rose and fell with his breath; his skin warmed her hand where she touched him. She'd never had a man spend the night in this house and she was surprised how happy it made her to find him beside her. It wouldn't be too difficult to get used to.

Carefully she drew away from him but before she could get far, he grabbed her hand. "Don't go. I like having you wrapped around me." He turned and kissed her hand.

"I was just going to put on some coffee."

In a voice thick with desire, he said, "Later," and gathered her into his arms.

By the time she'd showered, dressed and gone downstairs, a summer storm had come up and she dodged raindrops retrieving the paper. Back inside, she put coffee on, pulled out a frozen coffee cake and a container of raspberries, seeded and sliced a cantaloupe. From her new iPod Pink Martini's "Everywhere" started playing as she was getting mugs down prompting her to sing along.

"You're happy this morning," Tony said, coming down the steps, dressed for work.

"It's a beautiful day." She got plates from the cabinet and silverware from the drawer as she talked.

He stopped her from bustling by taking her in his arms. "It's raining, Margo."

"I've learned to like rain since I moved to Portland."

"Ah, that must be it. Couldn't be anything else, could it?" The timer on the microwave buzzed and she broke free of his arms to take the coffee cake out. "So, no answer to that question. Change the subject. Got it." He looked around the living room. "I didn't pay attention to much of your house last night. I like it."

She kept her eyes on the plate she was putting on the table. "We didn't spend a whole lot of time downstairs, did we?"

"All I noticed was that it looks like a little house in the woods floating on the water."

"That's exactly why I fell in love with it the first time I saw it."

He scanned the downstairs. A couch covered in a floral print, reading lamps at both ends and soft throws tossed over the back, and two chairs upholstered in a deep red fabric made up the living area. The dining table had four un-matched chairs around it upholstered in the same red as their bigger relatives in the living room. On the walls were hand-woven hangings, on the floor, vivid Persian-style carpets. Floor-to-ceiling shelves crammed with books filled one end of the room and a wood-burning, freestanding stove provided warmth when needed in a kitchen that featured open shelves piled with handmade pottery dishes.

"After your calm, uncluttered apartment, this must look like the back room of a Goodwill to you," she said.

He laughed. "No, it's comfortable, like a nest. It feels like you belong here."

"There's a guest room back there—" she nodded her head toward a hall near the stairway, "—and a small guest bath. Upstairs is my office as well as a deck with a view of the river and the interstate bridge."

He poured two cups of coffee, added milk to one he then handed to her. "I was out on the deck before I came downstairs. Who's the old guy next door? He was watching me pretty close."

"That's Mr. Todd. He takes it as his responsibility to look out for me. Tomorrow, before we go to the Gorge, I'll introduce you. In the meantime," she put a platter of raspberries and cantaloupe on the table with the coffee cake, "is this enough breakfast for you? I have some juice, too, and may be able to scare up some cereal but . . . "

"It's fine. You don't have to fuss over me."

"I want to. I like having you here."

He cut a piece of coffee cake and put it on a plate for her. "Good. Because I like being here."

*

Saturday morning after breakfast, Margo led Tony down to the end of the dock to show off her river. He stood behind her, his arms around her, as she waxed eloquent on the advantages of living on the water.

"Your Columbia River is beautiful but I've seen rivers before. It's that I'm interested in." He pointed to the mountain standing sentinel to the east, its top third covered in snow. "That sure puts what we call mountains in the East into a different perspective."

"That's Mt. Hood. Some places in Portland you can see Mt. Hood, Mt. Adams, Mt. St. Helens and, on a really clear day, a little bit of Mt. Rainier."

"Mt. St. Helens? The volcano that erupted?"

"They're all volcanoes."

"Makes it even more interesting."

Holding hands, they walked back down the dock toward Margo's house—and Mr. Todd. Her neighbor was waiting at the open door to his house next door. In a starched white dress shirt and dark trousers with knife-sharp creases, he still looked like the corporate lawyer he once was. He was only about five-feet-four inches tall, with a full head of neatly combed white hair and eyes the color of a faded blue work shirt. But there was nothing faded about the careful way he watched the couple as they approached his house. Margo was sure they'd been under his surveillance from the time they'd walked down the dock.

He greeted Margo with an affectionate hug. "Good morning, Margo. Nice to see you haven't run off to work on a Saturday." He turned to Tony. "And who's this with you?"

Making the introductions Margo added, "Tony's here on police business. He'll be around off and on for the next week or so."

"I hope you enjoy your visit, young man. And that you get to see more of our lovely state than just downtown Portland."

"In fact, we're going to the Gorge for the weekend," Margo said.

"Your favorite place. Good. You deserve a weekend off." He looked at Tony. "Detective, was it? Alessandro, can I have a few words with you before you go?"

Tony shot Margo a puzzled look but said only, "Of course, sir," and followed Mr. Todd into his house. Margo went home to finish her packing.

About five minutes later Tony came in the front door. "That was interesting."

"What did he want?"

"It was like Thursday night with your friend Liz, only she was more subtle."

"Liz? Subtle? I don't think I've never heard those two words in the same sentence before."

"Well, she was, at least relatively. Mr. Todd flat out warned me that if I do anything to hurt you, I'd have to answer to him. I told him I've known you all my life and would never hurt you. I think he believed me. I'm not sure. "

"Told you he looked after me."

"I tried to polish my image by telling him I was here with the FBI working on a case of national importance. Think that'll work?"

"Absolutely. After a lifetime of corporate law, he seems to find criminal law exciting. He's always asking about my cases."

"After my experiences with Liz and Mr. Todd, I'd say my family went easy on you, Keyes. Does everyone you know interrogate the men in your life like this?"

She picked up her duffle bag. "You packed?"

"Yes. You're not going to answer that question either, are you?"

"You catch on quick, Alessandro."

Up in the parking lot, as Margo opened the back of her Forester, Tony said, "Maybe you'll answer this one: do you ski on Mt. Hood?"

"I don't ski anyplace. If you're asking about the rack on top of my car, it could hold skis with the right attachments but the gizmos I have make it a bike rack for my mountain bike."

"Jesus, what the hell kind of big city Easterner am I? I fall for someone who lives in the water, owns a four-wheel drive and a mountain bike and spends her free time hiking around in a wilderness." He looked as if he was rethinking his taste in women.

Her retort was sharp and quick. "Yeah? Well, what kind of Northwesterner am I when I'm in love with a guy who probably doesn't even own a pair of hiking boots?"

He caught what was buried in the sentence. "So, you're in love with me."

"I didn't say that."

"Yeah, you did." Neither he nor the beaming expression on his face moved.

"Get in the car, Tony. Just get in the damn car."

With the passing of the shower, the weather began to cooperate with Margo's plans to show Tony her favorite place in all of the Northwest, the spectacular gorge the Columbia River cut through the Cascade Mountains millennia ago.

Stopping at Crown Point, high above the river on the old highway, they could see for miles upstream and down. Below them, wind-surfers and kite-boarders darted like dragonflies around the occasional barge and towboat convoy. Above, white clouds and the remains of their more sullen relatives that had dispensed rain earlier moved east, occasionally snagging on the tips of trees on the distant hills as if reluctant to leave town.

Pointing out a bald eagle soaring overhead, Margo asked if he could ever imagine that sight in Philadelphia. Tony replied that the only Eagles he'd ever seen in Philly played in the NFL since he was sure, when the starlings and pigeons moved into Center City, the flying kind had relocated to a better neighborhood.

After fighting through the crowds to climb for a close-up of Multnomah Falls and then hiking on one of Margo's favorite trails, they crossed the Bridge of the Gods to the Washington side of the river and checked into the hotel where Margo had a reservation for the night. They had a swim in the mineral pool and a long, leisurely dinner, then headed to their room where they planned to end the day with a soak in the hot tub on the balcony.

*

Tony took the hotel robes out to the deck, draped them over the railing to give them some privacy and climbed into the hot tub. When Margo had doused all the lights in the room, she joined him, wrapped in a towel, which she dropped onto the deck as she stepped into the water. God, she was beautiful. She looked like Venus or whoever it was in that painting rising from the sea. Except she was getting into the water. Not out of it.

What the hell was wrong with him? A beautiful naked woman was cuddling up against him and he was thinking about a goddamn painting.

They sat in silence for a while, the hot tub jets gently massaging them. Finally, Margo said, "This is just about perfect, isn't it? The smell of the trees, the stars . . . "

"Took us long enough to get here."

Her head popped up. "I'm sorry. Was the drive too long?"

"I didn't mean to get to the hotel. I meant to get naked in a hot tub." He settled her back on his shoulder.

"Oh, that." She laughed.

"Did you ever think about it before this summer?"

"Getting naked with you? Uh-huh. Did you?"

He kissed the side of her head. "Other than when I was in high school and thought about fucking every girl I saw who wasn't related to me?"

"Oh, great. I was part of the cast of hundreds in your teenaged fantasies. Just what every girl wants to hear." Crossing her arms over her breasts, she drew back from him, trying to look angry.

"I didn't say that was the only time, did I?" He pulled at her to get her back into his arms. "Since Mary Ellen's wedding, I've thought about it a lot."

"That's better." She returned to him. "We really blew it at Mary Ellen's wedding, didn't we? What exactly was the emergency that Noah dragged you off to take care of?"

"No emergency. Just saying good-bye to a couple of relatives. His mother had sent him to find me. He couldn't look at me for weeks afterwards without a silly grin on his face. Seeing your uncle with his hands on the ass of a wedding guest while they kiss was probably more than a twelve-year-old should know about his godfather."

"What did Catherine say?"

"Apparently he didn't tell his mother because she hasn't said anything. And I'm pretty sure she would have said something if she knew."

"Pretty sure? She'd have had your head on a pike if she's the same Catherine I knew."

He laughed. "She is. Believe me." He kissed the tip of her nose.

She sighed against his chest. "I guess it just wasn't meant to be. At least not then."

"Oh, yeah, after fifteen years we needed another eight months to make it work out." He shook his head and splashed her. "If I didn't love you so much, I'd be pissed that you didn't stick around."

"Do you really? Love me so much, I mean."

He kissed her temple. "Yeah, I do."

"Good." She put her arm across his chest and looked up at him. "I'm not big on unrequited love."

"Is this your way of telling me you love me?" This time he kissed her mouth.

When he pulled away, she made a little sound of disappointment and tried to bring his mouth back to hers. He shook his head. "Nope. Not 'til you say it."

"If I do, will you kiss me again?"

"Try me."

She kissed along his jaw line over to his ear and whispered, "I love you, Tony."

"There. That wasn't so tough, was it?" He stood up and reached for her hand. "Now, how 'bout we take this inside?"

"Hey, you said you'd kiss me."

"No, I didn't. But if we go inside, you might get lucky." He sat on the edge of the hot tub, pulled her into his lap and swung his legs over onto the balcony deck.

"What are you doing?" she asked.

"Taking this inside, counselor," he said as he picked up her towel and threw it over her.

She tried to get off his lap, but he wouldn't let her go. When she stopped struggling, he stood up with her in his arms and carried her into their room.

"You do know I can walk, don't you?" she said.

"Yeah, but I'm kinda liking this carrying-you-off-to-bed thing." He started to drop her on the bed.

"Tony! Don't, I'm dripping wet. Let me dry off."

"That sounds like fun. I'll do it." He set her down and took the towel from her, quickly wiped off his chest and her back, then pulled her against him. As he stroked her breasts with the towel, he slowly moved his stiffening erection against the cleft of her bottom and nibbled on her neck. "Isn't this better than just toweling off?" She sighed and tried to turn around. "Not yet. Only half done," he said as he gently rubbed the towel down to her hips, kissing her shoulders and the back of her neck as he caressed her. She moaned, put her hand over his and tried to move it down between her thighs, but he stopped her. "You're always in such a hurry, sugar."

She put her hands behind her, on his hips, as he massaged her body, ran his tongue around the edge of her ear, nipped at her earlobe. Finally he reached over, pulled down the spread and sheets, lifted her onto the bed and settled her on her back. She held out her arms to him but he ignored the invitation. Instead he separated her legs and positioned himself between her bent knees. Holding onto her hips he began to kiss her belly, circling her navel, finally moving down so he could make love to her with his mouth.

On a sharp intake of breath, she said, "Tony," and grasped his head.

He looked up at her. "You don't like it? Do you want me to stop?"

"Oh, God, no. Please don't stop."

Her hips bucked up at his mouth, her breathing became shallow and rapid as his tongue flicked over the nerve center hidden in the folds between her legs. When he substituted his thumb and introduced two fingers into her now-wet passage, she moaned, writhing in rhythm with his hand until she cried out in release.

He kissed his way back up her body, beginning with the insides of her thighs, up to her breasts, then her neck, her jaw, her cheeks. He took his time getting to her lips. As he reached her mouth, he entered her. She wrapped her arms and legs around him and devoured his mouth, nipping at his lips with her teeth, playing chase games with his tongue, riding along with him as they crested the wave of feeling and came down the other side.

Chapter 14

They drove home on the winding and curvy Highway 14 on the Washington side of the river, avoiding the freeway, trying to make their escape last as long as they could. But eventually they pulled into the marina parking lot. It was raining again, the gray sky reflecting Margo's mood now that the weekend was over.

Anxious to get into the house, they ran down the dock. When Margo was almost at her front door, the broken shards of a pot, crushed flowers and mounds of dirt scattered along the dock stopped her cold. She stepped back, almost tripping Tony who was close behind her.

"My front door's open," she whispered, "and there's a mess on the deck."

He moved in front of her. "I'll go see what's going on." He walked quietly up to the door and kicked it completely open. "Police. Don't move."

She stood just outside the door while he scanned the living area. There was no sign anyone had been there. "I'm going around to the deck and take a look up there," he said. "Stay outside. Do you have your cell phone?"

She nodded.

"If you see or hear anything unusual, call 9-1-1."

A few seconds later, Tony yelled, "Make that call, Margo. We need police and an ambulance. Mr. Todd's been hurt."

As she made the emergency call, Margo ran to the narrow walkway between their homes. In the wreckage of several more broken pots and damaged foliage was a crumpled heap—Mr. Todd with Tony kneeling beside him.

"Oh, God, is he . . . ?"

"He's got a good pulse in his neck but there's a bad gash in his head and he's not responding." He stroked her arm. "He'll be okay, sugar. Go back out front so you can let the EMTs in."

Minutes later, two patrolmen arrived along with an ambulance. While the EMTs took Mr. Todd away on a stretcher, Tony was on the phone with Sam Richardson. After he finished the call, he joined the police officers in talking to the neighbors.

Restless and wanting to do anything other than just wait, Margo called Mr. Todd's daughter to tell her what happened. After she hung up, she waited for the three cops to return.

But it was Sam and Tony who appeared at her front door. The two patrol officers had left with little to go on other than the information that neighbors had heard an outboard motor near the boat slip under her deck. No one had seen anything.

"Sam, why're you here?" Margo asked when the two men came in the front door.

"Because I don't believe in coincidences. Sit down. We need to talk."

Oh, hell, Margo thought. *There was that sentence again.*

"Tony's wasn't the only call I got today regarding you, Ms. Keyes. Your office was ransacked. When my boss heard from your boss, he called me," Sam said.

"Why'd they call you? And what's that have to do with this? I can't explain what happened in my office but why isn't this just somebody looking for an easy target to rob?"

"Who happened to pick on your house out of all the houses here? You don't have the most expensive looking house on the block and it's not the first one you come to if you come in by water."

"Okay, so what do you think it is?"

"I think—we think—someone is looking for something. Something he—she—believes you have. So, counselor, the question is what would that be?"

"What could I have? Depositions? Records of plea bargains? Even

I wouldn't break into anyone's office for that shit. Besides, what have I been involved in recently that's even vaguely interesting?"

Sam stared hard at her face, causing her to rub the whisker burns on her chin. Then he looked at Tony, who shrugged his shoulders with an "I tried my best" expression that bordered on a smirk.

"Oh, for God's sake you two, I meant in my professional life."

"Maybe you've been involved in something but don't know it." He turned to Tony again. "I was going over your files from the Jameson case yesterday. You remember the name of Frank Jameson's new girlfriend?"

"Brandy something. Last name's a president—Johnson? Ford?"

"The one in between. Nixon. Brandy Nixon. The woman we found dead in Forest Park in possession of Margo's messenger bag. You flew to Philadelphia with Frank Jameson and from Seattle to Portland with his girlfriend, Margo."

"Why would that coincidence be of interest to anyone?"

"Maybe someone doesn't think it's a coincidence. The other piece of information you need is that a man went out to the airport with Brandy Nixon's employee ID and tried to retrieve her briefcase. I don't know how he knew it was there—maybe she told him about the swap before she was killed—but the agent said he had a foreign accent, maybe Russian. He was told you had taken it to the police."

"Doesn't that look like I don't know what's in the bag?"

"I see what you're getting at, Sam," Tony said. "The feds think Jameson was trying to peddle Microsoft information. We didn't find anything on him or in his briefcase. But what did you tell us you heard him say in the Portland airport, Margo?"

"If you don't want it I know someone who does," Margo replied.

"Which sounds like he was playing two people off against each other—maybe the competing Russians. He flies to Philly, meets with one guy, gets himself killed. Nixon gets the news, tries to do the deal herself. She flies to Portland. In both cases, you're with them. Yes, you turned the bag into the airline, but you came and got it back."

Sam continued, "You could have removed what you wanted before you handed it in to me. Whoever did Nixon had already been played. Not hard to see why they might think they were being played again."

"Why do you think she was involved?" Margo asked. "I didn't find anything in her messenger bag that looked like Microsoft information."

"No, but, she did work with Jameson at Microsoft and, just before he moved in with her, quit her job. Told her friends she was about to be financially set for life. They thought she meant she and Jameson were getting married."

"Did you empty the bag when you got it home?" Tony asked.

"Sure, once I saw it wasn't mine, I looked for ID, went through it all. There was a wallet, some make-up, a cell phone, pens, breath mints, lint; the usual junk a woman carries around. No Microsoft documents."

"I doubt it would be paper, Margo. More likely a disc, something like that."

"We should find out what Jameson and Nixon were working on and some idea of what it would take to steal it. Might give us some idea what we're looking for. We can talk about all this tomorrow, Tony. You staying here?"

Tony looked to Margo for the answer. "Yes," she said, "he's staying here with me."

"Good. That'll give you an extra layer of security. I have a patrol car swinging by here regularly and the Multnomah County Sheriff's boat will be cruising the marina. Jeff's got the courthouse on alert so I think we have you covered."

"Like a blanket. All that makes me feel claustrophobic."

"Get used to it, counselor. You've got a whole new set of best friends until we get this figured out. The chief doesn't like Jeff's deputies being harassed."

*

After dinner, Tony volunteered to do the dishes while Margo checked in again with Mr. Todd's daughter. She said her father was doing much better. He'd told the police that about the time he expected to see Margo and Tony return from the Gorge, he noticed a tall, dark-haired man jiggling the door at Margo's house. Thinking it was Tony having trouble with the lock that he knew could be tricky, he went out to help. He immediately saw it was a teenaged stranger who managed to get the door jimmied just as Mr. Todd reached him.

Her neighbor started back for his own house to call the police, but the kid grabbed him and dragged him to the side walkway. He didn't remember much after that.

He was being held overnight for observation but would probably be discharged the next day and would be at his daughter's house for a couple days after that. Relieved that his injuries weren't any more serious, Margo sent him her love and promised to visit him the next evening.

After the phone call, Margo settled on the couch. Rearranging pillows to make herself more comfortable, she knocked something from behind one onto the floor. When she picked it up, she didn't recognize it.

"Tony, is this yours?" she asked, holding up a slim red flash drive.

"No, isn't it yours?"

She shook her head. "

Tony took it from her, turned it over in his hand a couple times. "When was the last time you cleaned?"

"Why are you interested in my housekeeping habits? Looking for a maid?"

There was no humor in his eyes.

"Okay, it was right before I went back to Philly." She shrugged and half smiled. "I always leave the house clean in case I don't come back and someone else has to pack it up."

"Sounds like the Margo I know and love. And you said you emptied Nixon's messenger bag out . . . did you do it in here?"

They looked at each other for a moment or two then Margo gestured to him to follow her to her office. She booted up her computer and they inserted the flash drive. On it were two files: one was labeled "Office Suite Beta Version" and the other "Body Bot Beta," which appeared to be a body-sensitive game.

"Now we can deal," Tony said. "All we have to do is find out who we're dealing with."

Chapter 15

"Do you ever come up for air?" the tall, dark and familiar man standing in the door of her office asked.

"What time is it?" She'd been working so intently the afternoon had slid into evening and she hadn't even noticed.

"It's about seven-thirty." Tony said. "I'm ready for dinner."

She was just about to turn off her computer when she heard the "bing" that meant she had a new email message. Out of habit, she opened it. She didn't find the run-of-the-mill business she expected.

"Tony, look at this." She pointed to the computer screen.

The message was from someone named Viktor Smirnov. It said: "*You have something that belongs to me. I don't care who you are, if you don't return it, you will find yourself in the same place as your colleagues who attempted to play games with me.*"

"Looks like another Russian has come to the party," Tony said.

"Or someone without imagination who wants us to think he's Russian. A vodka brand as his alias? Really?" Margo said.

"Let's see if he's still there." Tony typed a response. A reply came back. He typed again. Viktor answered.

"He says he knows you have the two programs your colleagues passed on to you before he took care of them for going back on their deal." He typed again. "I'm asking what's in it for you since whatever he gave to Jameson and Nixon didn't include you. He offered fifty thousand dollars."

"Hell, I'll sell him Kiki for that." She watched as Tony negotiated back and forth for several more messages. "What now?"

"We settled on $100,000 and I'm waiting for him to tell me what the terms are."

The message that came back this time was longer than the others. There were a dozen conditions for the exchange of the material. The list began with a date a week away and a place. "No cops, no witnesses, no weapons" ended the list.

"You're not meeting him alone," Tony said as he responded.

"What if that's the only way?"

"We'll find some other way. You're not meeting him alone."

She decided not to argue with the tone of voice he was using and the set of his face.

Eventually, Tony negotiating as Margo got Viktor to agree she could bring her boyfriend with her to the Chinook picnic shelter in Blue Lake Park at 10 p.m. in a week. When Tony asked where that was, Margo shuddered and told him it was about five minutes from her house. He didn't say anything but put his arm around her and hugged her before he pulled out his cell phone and called Sam.

*

"Your eye candy's here," Kiki said, swinging on the doorjamb into Margo's office.

"He's here so we can drive home. And Kiki, I appreciate how gorgeous he is, but . . ."

"Who's gorgeous? You?" Tony materialized at the door. She had to agree with Kiki. He *was* eye candy. He'd swapped his gray suit and maroon tie for a version of Northwest business casual—jeans and a jacket with a white shirt and tie—which almost made him a match for Sam Richardson, who never wore anything but jeans although Tony hadn't gone so far as to buy cowboy boots. Yet.

Kiki smiled. "*Buon giorno, detectivo.*"

"*Buon pomeriggio, Kiki. Come sieta?*"

"Sorry, haven't gotten that far in my online Italian lessons."

"I said good afternoon and asked how you are."

"I'm fine, *grazie*. Maybe you have time today to help me with my Italian? The website I found doesn't really tell you the good stuff. Like how to swear."

"*Maledizione. Figlio di puttana. Merda. Vaffanculo,*" Margo said.

"What's all that mean?" Kiki asked.

Tony started to answer but Margo interrupted. "Look it up on a translation website. Here, I'll write them down for you." She grabbed a piece of paper and wrote as she finished speaking. "But do the translating on your own time, *per favore.* On county time, I need those citations I asked for. *Andiamo.*"

"Who knew you could speak Italian, too? Must be trying to impress you, Tony." Kiki patted him on the arm and disappeared in the general direction of her desk.

"So, you're trying to impress me?" Tony asked.

"Do I have to, *detectivo?*"

"No, like I told Greer, you did that a long time ago, *avvocatessa.*"

"Good, because I have now exhausted all the Italian I can remember. Did you come to tell me you're ready to go home?"

"After you do one thing. I'm flying to Long Beach tomorrow for a couple of days to coordinate with them. Sam wants you to call him before we leave tonight so he can talk to you about extra security precautions while you're alone."

"Now what?" She squinted at him for a moment with her mouth pursed. "All this babysitting gives me a headache. And claustrophobia."

"He wants you to arm your security system for starters, even when you're in the house. I didn't know you had one."

"I only set it when I'm going to be gone for a long time."

"You didn't set it when we left for our weekend in the Gorge."

"I was distracted." She hoped to waylay him with a reference to why she had been distracted. It didn't work.

"He wants it on all the time."

She sighed. "I'm getting tired of this, Tony, but okay, I'll call and see what he wants." Before he could say anything else she added, "And I'll do what he asks."

Tony left to get the car and, as she punched in Sam's number, she heard Greer waylay him as he walked past her office, two doors away from Margo's. He didn't go in, only stood in the doorway so she heard some of the conversation. Greer appeared to ask him what he was up to in Portland, where he was staying, what he'd seen, where he'd been. That and a less-than-subtle attempt to find out what the relationship was between Margo and Tony.

Maybe Paul Dreier wasn't as irresistible as he thought he was.

Sam gave her instructions about making sure someone knew where she was when she wasn't at work and arming her security system. She "yes, Sam'd" him so much she was sure he was on the verge of doubting her sincerity.

He pointed out to her that Viktor's insistence on meeting with her the following week, not any sooner, was odd at best, downright dangerous at worst. It gave Viktor too much time to cause trouble. She reluctantly agreed.

Although she didn't tell him.

*

After dinner, Margo loaded the dishwasher while Tony packed for his trip to Long Beach. When he came back downstairs, he joined Margo on the couch. "I've been thinking," he began. "I've liked living with you and I . . . "

"A week isn't really living together, Tony."

"Well, okay, it isn't. But it feels right and I was wondering, maybe we should start thinking about . . . start talking about whether we want to do this on a more long-term basis."

"Do what? Live together?"

"We said we'd work things out as we went along and . . . "

"You're about to walk out the door for two days and you want to talk about living together?" Pulling away from him, she added, "Everything's been fine the way it is. You were the one who said we should just enjoy what we had and not try to overthink things."

"All I'm suggesting . . . "

"I know what you're suggesting. But I don't know why you're bringing it up now." She could feel tears beginning to form and she swallowed hard to keep them from falling.

"What's going on, Margo? Why're you crying?"

She moved to the farthest corner of the couch. "Okay, it's been good for the past week. But it's not real. Our real lives are three thousand miles apart. On top of that, we have careers with time schedules that don't mesh very well. I don't know if we can even find jobs in the same place."

"Those are the same things about geography and careers you've brought up before, things we can work at fixing. I don't buy that's what's bothering you. What's this really about?"

She was silent, twisting a ring on her right hand, not looking at him. Finally she did. "Do you remember much about the year of my father's trial?"

"Your father's trial? What does that have to do with . . . ?"

"What my father did always has something to do with how I look at things, Tony, don't you know that? It was an awful year, except for your kindness that summer."

"I don't remember being kind. I remember kissing a beautiful girl in a bikini."

"Great. You didn't take that any more seriously than you're taking this."

"This is how I take things seriously, Margo. I thought you knew . . . "

"Okay, you're taking it seriously. It's another one of those things that keep tripping me up. Somehow I keep expecting you to be, I don't know, like . . . "

"You?"

"Maybe that's part of it. We approach things so differently. I think everything through from every angle before I make a decision. You jump in. You had this amazing family life growing up. I had none to speak of and ran away from what I did have like I was being chased by demons from hell."

"You left Philly because of your family? I thought you wanted to see what the West Coast was like."

"I didn't leave Philly. I escaped. I gave up Yale and Columbia and Princeton and every place I was accepted to go to college, the places I'd dreamed of going all through high school, to go to the University of Washington, so I could get away from being Kenny Keyes' daughter. From being Daisy Keyes."

"Who the hell is Daisy Keyes?"

"That's what my grandmother called me. That's who I pictured myself as. Daisy Keyes was a sad nothing, powerless over her own life, at the mercy of the people around her who were in control—my father, the prosecutors, the press."

She ran her hand through her hair and looked directly at him. "I killed Daisy on that plane to Seattle and swore I'd always be in control of my life. And I've made good on that promise." She dropped her eyes. "I won't go back to being Daisy again. Not for anyone. Not even for you."

"Go back to being Daisy? What in God's name are you talking about?"

After a long pause, she answered. "At first I thought this feeling was just a reaction to kissing you, making love with you. But now it's more like . . . like . . . events spinning out of control, things running away with me. All I can imagine is selling my house, changing my job, losing my name, losing my career, being responsible for kids if we have them. Not being in control of my life again. And I'm afraid."

"Afraid? Of me?"

"No, of course I'm not afraid of you. I'm afraid of what loving you means."

"But we've never talked about any of that and I've certainly never asked you to do any of those things."

"I know you haven't. But isn't that what happens when people pair up? Get serious? Isn't that what people expect?" She stared at her hands, clenched into fists.

"People, Margo? Or you overthinking everything. Running it into the ground." He ran his thumb back and forth across his mouth. Finally, he said, "I'm not sure what to say. Most of what I can think of would probably make it worse. So, I'll just ask one question." He shook his head. "I'm not sure I'll like the answer but—do you want us to be together when I get back?"

She kept her eyes down. "I don't know what I want other than to stop feeling afraid."

"That's the answer then." He stood up. "I'll be in Long Beach for the next two days. When I come back, I'll check into the Marriott where the other guys are staying. Should I call you?"

"If you still want to."

He didn't respond, but ran the steps to the second floor. He returned with his suitcase.

"Tony . . ." She finally looked at him, at his back, as he opened the front door. "I've hurt you and I didn't mean to. I didn't. It's just that . . . "

"I know you didn't mean to, Margo. But you did." Without looking back, he slammed the door and was gone.

Chapter 16

"No, Kiki, that's not what I asked for. I asked for the depositions on the Smithson case. This is the Smythden . . . "

"I'm sorry. I should have asked you to write it down. They sound alike." Kiki snatched the file from Margo's outstretched hand. "Jeesh. I'll be glad when Tony's back and your disposition improves."

"I wouldn't count on that happening." Margo busied herself with her computer.

"What's that mean?"

"I don't want to talk about it."

"Oh, 'cause that always helps, not talking about it."

"Just get me the right file, please."

Kiki opened her mouth to respond but the phone rang and Margo shooed her out of the office and answered it.

"I need you over here, counselor," Sam Richardson said. "Tony's back and we have to get things set up for the meeting with Viktor."

"Sam, can't you do it without me, maybe find an officer who looks like me and let her meet him?"

"Viktor apparently knows who you are. He expects Margo Keyes, not some police officer who's your height and weight."

"Then how about you doing it with me? He won't . . . "

"He gave you a yard-long list of requirements to make this happen including who you could bring. If we change anything, he'll bolt and you know it. Look, I don't care what's going on in your personal life. I only want two things. First, I want you to get your ass over here so we can get this taken care of. And second, I'd like you to act like the professional I know you are."

"When?"

"When do I want you to act like a grown-up?"

"When do you want me over there?"

"Half an hour work?"

"I'll be there."

*

The room where they were to meet was empty when she got there. Less than five minutes later, Tony walked in. He stopped in the doorway when he saw her. She was sure the expression on her face reflected how nervous she was.

"Hi," she said. She hated how her voice quivered. "How was Long Beach?"

He dropped a notebook on the table at the opposite end from where she was sitting. "Didn't see much of it except the port and police headquarters."

"Did it help with what you're working on?"

"Some."

The arrival of Sam and Danny along with a few other members of the task force relieved her of having to think of something else to say.

"Okay, people, let's get this organized," Sam said. Most of the task force members were clustered near Sam. Only Margo and Tony were at the ends of the table. He glanced at them. "Could one of you move so I don't have to look back and forth like I'm watching a tennis match?" After a few seconds, both Tony and Margo got up and moved to chairs directly across from him. "That's better. Tony, anything from Long Beach we should know?"

"I know why he put off meeting with Margo. He was in Long Beach to meet with a guy who'd agreed to sell Genentec information. Guy got cold feet at the last minute and went to the FBI. They taped his conversation arranging the handover. But

Viktor never showed." His eyes slid over to Margo, then went back to Sam. "This morning I heard from Long Beach. They found the Genentec source. Shot."

"Christ, this guy piles up bodies like hay bales. Margo, I want to know where you are this weekend and I'm upping the patrols out on Marine Drive."

"For once, I agree with you, Sam."

"Okay, what Tony just told us makes it even more important that we take him down on Monday. Margo, you know what you're supposed to do. Tony, you're not supposed to come armed but I want a weapon in there with you. He'll ask you to get rid of it but at least it'll be within reach."

"Where'll you be, Sam?" Margo asked.

"Across Marine Drive in that industrial site. I'm concerned that it's not an easy place to get buttoned down. He can see anyone on Marine Drive and the neighborhood to the south is a rabbit warren where we can hide, but we can't see a fucking thing in the park."

"No place in the park itself to stash a few cops?" Tony asked.

"We'll have a couple guys out there dressed as county maintenance men but I'd be willing to bet he'll have the park swept by some of his folks before he decides to go there himself."

"Then how're you going to get him, Sam?" Margo asked.

"Tracer on the key ring with the flash drive. We'll follow him when he leaves. As soon as you do the swap, you and Tony get the hell out of there. Let us take care of the rest."

"I have no intention of hanging around," Margo said.

As they walked out the door of the meeting room, Sam said, "Now all I have to do is find a way to get a reporter to sit on a story."

"I have a couple good contacts at the *Oregonian*, can I help?" Margo said.

"It's not the Big O. It's *Willamette Week*. A story about Russian mobster and gang activity in Portland is about to come out and it could make Viktor nervous enough to be a no show."

"I can talk to Fiona, if you'd like."

"Amanda tried but it was a no-go. But, sure, you can try. Just be careful what you tell her."

"Before I call her, I'll talk to Jeff, see what advice he has. Maybe you can check with your boss, too. Ask Chris if we can tell her we'll talk to her before anyone else when it's wrapped up so they're first on the web with the story."

"Sure, fine. I'll see what L.T. says and call Jeff."

After it was all cleared with the Police Bureau and the DA's office, Margo called Fiona.

"Margo," she said, "is this important or can I get back to you? I'm on deadline for a big story."

"I think it's your story I want to talk to you about."

There was a momentary silence. "You don't know what I'm working on, do you?"

"About it an hour ago I heard that *Willamette Week* was about to break a story on Russian mob activities and their connection with Russian gangs here. It sounded like something you'd be working on. Are you?"

Another silence. "Why're you interested? It doesn't connect with any of your cases, does it?"

"Nothing that I'm prosecuting, no, but, remember at the gallery? I said Tony was here on business? We were vague about it because we didn't want two reporters sniffing around just yet. But there's a big story in this, the kind that wins prizes."

"Why do you keep saying 'we'? How're you involved?"

Now it was Margo's turn to be silent for a moment. "Okay, listen, this is so far off the record, you can't see the record with a telescope. Promise?"

Fiona laughed. "Okay, girlfriend. I promise."

"I'm mixed up in it because I accidently swapped messenger

bags with someone on my way back from Philly. She ended up dead and the guy we're after, a Russian, thinks I have what she was trying to sell to him."

"And what's that?"

"Proprietary information from a big Northwest company. That's what this is all about, intellectual property theft . . . industrial espionage."

"I'm writing about Russian gangs. But I've gotten an earful about the Russian mob. Are they the ones doing the dirty work?"

"Yeah, they're also responsible for, shall we say, eliminating inconvenient people. Two back East, another couple in California. Sam Richardson has one here . . . "

"The Nike guy? So that's what Amanda was hinting around about. I couldn't figure it out."

"Well, I'm going to come right out and ask—can we get you to hold the story? We might be close to getting the guy who's the local contact with the Russian mob but if your piece hits the streets, it could blow us out of the water. And, not that I'm trying to guilt you into doing it, but I have a big fat target on my back because the guy thinks I have something he wants."

"Right. Not that you're trying to guilt me into anything."

"Seriously, is there any way you can back-burner your story? Give us room to maneuver and I promise you I'll talk to you first when it's settled and you'll get first crack at the Portland Police Bureau team, too."

"This is way beyond my pay grade. I'll have to talk to my editor. But if he agrees, you'll owe me, big time. Trying to fill that news hole won't be fun."

"I know. I don't know how, but I'll make it up to you. I promise."

Margo was home when Fiona called to report her editor had said he was inclined to err on the side of publication but he'd talk to his publisher and get back to them. Margo thanked her profusely and gave Fiona Sam's phone number.

Half an hour later, Sam called to report success. Ben Stein had reluctantly agreed to hold the story. But if he found out another paper was on the verge of breaking it, he was running it online. It was the best he could offer. Sam took the deal.

Margo was about to hang up when Sam said, "Your friend's not a lot of fun to be around right now. How're you doing?"

She sighed. "I'm all right, I guess."

"Amanda says if you need a sympathetic ear, give her a call. She's good at keeping her mouth shut and her ears open. That last was me talking, not her."

"I appreciate the offer."

"You haven't asked for any but I'm going to give you a piece of advice, counselor. When you have something good, hold on to it. Doesn't come along very often. Nothing was easy about us but we made it work. And, like I've said, if Amanda and I could make it happen . . . "

"Anyone can. I remember. Thanks, Sam."

Chapter 17

Saturday morning Margo decided if she was going to survive the weekend without Tony, she had to do one of two things: work or clean. She'd cleared her desk to keep from thinking about him all week so that left cleaning.

Lots of upbeat music would help. She put on two Alicia Keys CDs and started a load of laundry. The towels in the bathroom with remnants of Tony's shaving gel and soap went into the washer along with the sheets and the pillowcase that smelled of his cologne. A shirt he'd left got buried in a drawer so she wouldn't see it every time she opened the closet.

By the time she finished scrubbing, vacuuming and washing, her stomach was growling. The yogurt and English muffin she'd eaten for breakfast were long gone and she decided an omelet sounded good. But when she opened the refrigerator to get the eggs, she found the leftover marinara sauce Tony'd made, the wine he liked, the cheese he'd picked out for her to try. On the counter was the cereal he ate for breakfast.

Shit. She was back where she started.

She poured the last of the pot of coffee and called Fiona.

"You still speaking to me?" she asked when her friend answered.

"Of course. Turns out it wasn't as hard as I expected to fill the news hole. The guy who was next week's feature had it already to go. I think he's after my job but right now, I don't care. I'm off the hook and ready to hear all the juicy details you promised for my big story."

"With luck, it'll be in a day or two." Margo paused. "I suppose you and Mark have plans for tonight."

There was a long silence. "Mark has plans. I don't. He's gone back to Seattle."

"For the weekend?"

"No, for good." Before Margo could ask more questions, Fiona said, "It's a long story. I'm not sure I can go through it right now. But why were you asking about my plans tonight?"

"I'm at loose ends and would like some company. Actually, I need a shoulder to cry on. You available?"

"Men. Honestly. Can't live without them. Can't make them behave so you can live with them." She sighed. "Why don't you come here? I have a nice bottle of pinot gris and I just put a pan of brownies in the oven. If you don't come over, I'll finish off both of them myself and feel awful in the morning. And bring what you need to spend the night."

Fiona lived in St. Johns, a neighborhood north of downtown Portland, in a one-story, Craftsman-style house, restored to its original beauty by her landlord. Margo loved visiting there. The only drawback was that she usually had to fight Pulitzer, Fiona's orange marmalade cat, for the leather lounge chair she liked, as well as the office/guest room where she would be sleeping because Pulitzer viewed both as hers.

This time, the cat seemed to know something was wrong because she vacated the chair as soon as Margo walked in and didn't scratch at her bag when Margo put it on the day bed in the guest room.

Fiona poured each of them a glass of wine, overriding Margo's objection that it was only four o'clock in the afternoon. They curled up in their respective places in the living room and sipped at the wine.

"Okay," Fiona said. "Who's first?"

Margo said, "I'll go. I have managed to screw up the best relationship I've had in years—maybe ever—because it scares me shitless." She related what had happened before Tony left for Long Beach and they dissected it for a while before Margo said, "Enough. I've been wallowing in this for days. Let's wallow in yours. What happened with Mark?"

"The long and short of it is that the whole time we were together here, he was seeing someone in Seattle. Now, they're getting married."

"What? How . . . "

"I don't know if you knew but he went back to Seattle every other weekend. To see his family, he said. He never said what family but I figured he went to see his parents. Turns out, he was visiting his daughter. And her mother."

"I didn't even know he'd been married."

"He was never married. His daughter was born right after he moved to Portland so for almost two years he's been maintaining two relationships a couple hundred miles apart. He's marrying the mother of his child, for his daughter's sake, he says."

"I guess I'm happy for the little girl but, Jesus, why the hell didn't he think of that before now?"

"I'm trying to believe I'm better off but I can't quite get there yet. And I feel used."

"I'd say you should feel lucky."

For the rest of the afternoon and on into the evening they went over every detail of their respective love lives ending up with Fiona saying, "Well, all I can say is, the results don't seem to turn out any different whether you have the right man or the wrong one. You have the right man. I had the wrong one but here we are, spending the weekend with each other and a pan of brownies." She took another square from the pan. "At least Tony adores you. I'd kill to have someone look at me the way he looks at you."

"Right now, the way he looks at me could be classified as a lethal weapon."

They finished the bottle of wine and made a salad for dinner to make up for eating an entire batch of brownies. After promising each other they would be more cheerful the next day, they went to bed early.

Pulitzer woke Margo at seven, so Margo got up and fed her. By the time her hostess came into the kitchen, she had a pot of coffee going and was reading the Sunday paper.

"How about we go out for brunch someplace?" Fiona suggested. "Maybe on the river?"

"I live on the river. How about Kenny and Zuke's?" Margo suggested. "I haven't been there in ages."

They showered, dressed and headed out in Fiona's car for downtown. After brunch, during which they didn't discuss their love lives at all, they headed back to Fiona's. Margo was packing her things so she could go home when her cell phone rang. It was Sam and he was pissed.

"Where the hell are you, counselor? You were supposed to let me know where you were."

"Sorry, Sam. I forgot."

"Don't do it again. I'm up to my ass in alligators and I don't need to be worrying about you."

"What's going on?"

"The kid who beat up Mr. Todd came back and . . . "

"Oh, Jesus, did he get hurt again?"

"He's fine. Mr. Todd saw him from inside his house this time, called 9-1-1 and we picked the kid up. He got bailed out five minutes after we brought him in but not before we confirmed he has Russian gang connections. I discovered you weren't home when I went to talk to Mr. Todd."

"I'm at Fiona's, in St. Johns."

"Stay there. It's easier to keep tabs on you there than at the marina."

After the phone call, Margo emailed Viktor: *"WTF? The cops told me a kid with Russian gang connections was responsible for trying to break into my house—again. You wouldn't know anything about that, would you? After all, we have a deal. Don't we?"*

Several hours later she got a response. While not apologizing, Viktor said he'd take care of the problem. She thanked him, turned off Fiona's computer and volunteered to make dinner.

Chapter 18

Monday morning Margo had a hard time concentrating on her work as she kept checking the time, thinking that in twelve, then ten, then eight hours, she'd be meeting a killer in Blue Lake Park. A phone call from Sam made it worse.

After he went through, one more time, the details of the evening, he added, "Oh, and the kid who beat up Mr. Todd's not a problem anymore. Drive-by shooting last night."

"Oh, Jesus. That's what he meant."

"That's what who meant?"

"When I emailed Viktor last night and asked him what the fuck was going on, he promised to take care of it. I had no idea . . . " She gulped hard.

"Margo, don't go all squishy on me here. The kid was on his way to becoming a statistic long before you emailed Viktor. And did you really ask him what the fuck?"

*

Margo left work early. She tried to take a nap but that didn't happen. Music didn't soothe her. She couldn't concentrate on a book. She was hungry but didn't know what she wanted to eat. Finally, she ate a container of yogurt and some toast and lost a couple hours online reading about the troubles of everyplace else in the world on Google News.

At quarter of ten, Tony rang from the security gate and she went up the ramp to join him. Silently they drove the five minutes it took to get to Blue Lake Park.

The only time Margo had been at the park in the evening was

for a long-ago summer concert when the place had been crowded with people and alive with music. Now, deserted of any visible human life, Blue Lake was silent and dark.

They parked just outside the barrier that closed off the park at night and walked the rest of the way. A half moon forced dim light through thick branches, casting shadows so inky she expected to leave footprints from walking through them. With no lights anywhere, even with the flashlight beam she swept across the road, it was like moving through an endless, silent tunnel.

Silent until a breeze moved through the branches like a soft hand, touching leaves, caressing needles, moving them around, one tree at a time, disturbing the night air.

As her eyes acclimated to the night, she began to see buildings looming over the grass that tonight looked like the haunts of serial killers or slasher movie villains. The only thing missing was the spooky music she began to hear in her head as soon as the thought occurred it was missing.

Tony walked with her to the edge of the grassy area where the picnic tables were and stopped. "You okay going through with this, Margo?"

She nodded.

"Don't take any chances. Make the exchange and get the hell away from him. I'll be right over there, waiting for you." She could hear worry in his voice. He hesitated for a moment, as if about to say something else—or to grab her and run—before turning and walking toward the picnic tables where Viktor had stipulated he wait.

She watched as Tony and the beam from his flashlight moved away from her. Alone now, without even the sound of his footsteps to keep her company, she began to doubt she'd given him an honest answer. Maybe she wasn't sure she wanted to do this. Maybe what she wanted to do was run back to her car.

Ahead of her the twists and turns of a kids' jungle gym emerged from the dark. Behind it was the picnic shelter. No one was visible there or anywhere else.

"Viktor?" she called. "It's Margo Keyes. I have what you want." She stopped about thirty yards from the picnic shelter. "Where are you? I want to see you."

There was no answer other than the trees protesting the breeze that disturbed them. But after the breeze stopped, she thought she could hear the sound of someone breathing. However, no one was visible when she played the light in the direction of the sound.

"I'm going to shine the flashlight over the picnic shelter," she said as she began to illuminate the picnic tables in front of the shelter.

"Don't do that, Miss Keyes. Focus your light on the ground." A man's voice with a heavy Russian accent came from deep inside the picnic shelter. "And have your friend put his weapon on the table nearest him. I'm sure he has one."

She turned toward the roadway. "Tony? Did you hear?"

"It's on the table," Tony called. She saw him shine his flashlight on the Glock he'd been carrying.

"Keep your light on the weapon, please," Viktor said. "Now, Miss Keyes, my merchandise. Place it . . . "

"First tell me why you killed that boy."

"You asked me to take care of it. I did. Now, put my merchandise on the table closest to you and illuminate it. When I see it, you'll get your money."

She put the flash drive on the picnic table and shone her flashlight on it.

"I thought you understood not to play games with me, Miss Keyes," Viktor said in an irritated voice. "I will give you exactly five seconds to put my merchandise on that table. I don't care who you are, you cannot get away with this."

"I *have* put it on the table. That's what I . . . "

"Five, four . . . " The sound of his voice was coming closer. "Three . . . two . . . "

He was beside her before she knew he was so close. "You should know better, Miss Keyes." He grabbed her and shook her so hard she dropped the flashlight.

Before Viktor could do anything else, she heard, "Let her go, you son of a bitch." Tony lunged at Viktor but the Russian anticipated him and shoved Margo in his direction before taking off. She stumbled in the grass, grabbing at Tony, tripping on his feet, falling, her face smacking the root of a tree, sending ribbons of pain through her nose and around her eyes.

"Are you all right?" Tony knelt beside her, scanning the dark with his light, trying to pick out the fleeing Viktor.

She attempted to stand. "I don't know. I think . . . " She never finished the sentence. Her knees buckled and she went back down onto the grass.

What happened next was a jumble she couldn't sort out, even later with a lot of effort. Tony barking orders, swearing in Italian and English, pacing. A gurney. An ambulance ride. Pain. Confusion.

The ER visit was clearer. After the doctor had seen her, manipulated her nose and packed it, the nurse cleaned the blood from her face and went to see if they were admitting her for observation.

Sam came in when the nurse left.

"Did you get him?" she asked.

"No, Tony lost him when he was trying to help you. My guys on Marine Drive never saw him. Viktor must have made his way back into the residential neighborhood south of the park. We had patrol cars there but there are a dozen different ways to get out."

"Shit." She grasped his arm and tried to pull herself up but a burst of pain fanned out over her face. "Oh, God, that hurts."

"The nurse'll be back in a minute. If they're sure you're not concussed, you can have a pain med."

"What're you doing here, anyway?" Margo said. "Why aren't you out there looking for Viktor?"

"Got people doing that. I get to babysit the banged-up DA."
He stared at her face for a few seconds. "Margo, since you're now
officially on Viktor's shit list, you're gonna need more security."

"Meaning?"

"Meaning I'm putting you in a hotel downtown where we can
keep an eye on you."

"Absolutely not. I won't be cooped up in a hotel room."

"You don't have a choice. I just talked to Lt. Angel. He says the
chief and Jeff have agreed that's how to handle this. Danny will
stay with you at night. I'll have someone walk you back and forth
to the courthouse and stay with you during the day."

"I won't . . . "

"You will." He had a look on his face that brooked no further
argument. "If they keep you overnight here, you'll have a police
guard at the door of your room. If they release you, I'll go with
you so you can pack up what you want to take with you."

"Can't I . . . ?"

"Sit in protective custody in a nice little jail cell? I understand
that was discussed. But they didn't think you'd like the food."

"Goddamn. Shit. Son of a bitch."

"That about sums it up, counselor."

*

They kept her overnight, but she showed no signs of concussion.
The next morning, the officer at the door of her hospital room
escorted her home and she packed up a week's worth of clothes
and went to work.

That's where she discovered her daytime security was Tony.
He sat outside her office door working on a laptop, interspersed
with conversations with all the women who walked by. He was
distracting. For the office, of course.

Her first opportunity to complain about her security detail

came that afternoon when she was summoned to Central Precinct to meet with Sam.

She didn't pay any attention to Tony hovering in the background when she got to Sam's desk. "What the hell are you thinking, Sam? I don't need a bodyguard or a babysitter in my office. No one's gonna get at me there."

"People with more experience than you have decided you do need a bodyguard, Margo. So, you've got one."

"Then why not assign Danny? She's with me at the hotel every night, why not at work?"

"I need her here. And, if you're this pleasant to her at the hotel, she deserves a break from being with you."

"I like you, Sam, I really do. But you're bossy and stubborn and you're . . ."

"In charge of this part of the investigation so let's go someplace with some peace and quiet and figure out what's next." He stood up from his desk and made a gesture indicating she was to follow him down the hall.

"I'm not going to win this, am I?" Margo said.

"Nope. And, FYI, I'm better at bossy and stubborn than you are, which might explain why it irritates you so much."

Margo pretended to ignore the grin on his face. And she refused to look at Tony who snorted at Sam's response.

Sam borrowed Lt. Angel's office, which was empty for the moment. After Danny arrived he started with, "So, where are we?"

"I got a message from Viktor I need to tell you about." Margo looked from Sam to Danny. "But first, no one's asked me why Viktor hasn't thought twice about dealing with me. Aren't you curious?"

"He thinks you're your father's daughter," Sam responded.

Margo felt her eyes widen. "How do you know about my father?"

"Same way Viktor does, I imagine. I Googled you."

"I've never seen anything about my father when I've Googled myself."

"Must not have gone back far enough. It was there when I looked last week. The feds and I wanted the answer to the question you just asked. I asked Jeff and he suggested I search online."

"What the fuck're you talking about?" Danny asked.

"My father was a lawyer, too, Danny. He had a private practice with a lot of little clients and one big one—the Philly mob. He died in a federal prison after being convicted on RICO charges. Tony's family lived next door to mine so he knows about it. But no one in Portland knows—well, I *thought* no one knew—except Jeff and he'd promised not to tell anyone. Viktor has hinted in the past that he knew and now, with this last email, he's blatant about it."

She handed Sam a copy of the message. *"You're playing a dangerous game. Being Kenny Keyes' daughter won't protect you. Follow these directions precisely or you'll pay the same price your two colleagues did."* It continued with a list of instructions on how to deliver his "merchandise" to a Russian grocery store in two days.

"Now what, Sam?" Margo asked.

"Now we have two days to figure out what he wants. Anyone have any bright ideas?" There was no response. He started pacing the floor. "Okay, what do we know? Two people were trying to sell something they'd stolen from Microsoft to Viktor and maybe to someone else in competing deals. We thought the flash drive was it, but Viktor says it isn't. He thinks Margo's holding out on him. Two people who crossed him are already dead, which puts a big, fat target on Margo's back. That's all we know. And it's jack shit."

He scrubbed his hands over his face as if to wash away his frustration. "I'm tired of what we don't know, can't find or didn't do right. We cannot fall on our asses again. It's too important and I don't like having the rug pulled out from under me this way."

Tony shook his head. "So, what do we do? All I can come up

with is tearing Jameson's and Nixon's bags apart. Literally. Maybe something's hidden there."

"That's all I can come up with, too," Sam said. "Can you get the Philly police or the feds to take Jameson's bag apart while we do hers?"

"Yeah, I'll do it now," Tony said and left the meeting to make the call.

"Danny, call the Redmond PD and ask them again what they found in Nixon's place. Maybe we overlooked something there."

"What can I do, Sam?" Margo asked.

"Answer Viktor's email. Stall him. Get us more time. Otherwise, you're going out to Beaverton with nothing to offer except your charm and those black eyes you're sporting."

Back in her office, Margo responded to Viktor's email. After a few negotiations that made her feel quite proud of herself, Viktor gave her one extra day. She emailed Sam about the extra day, omitting the other negotiations.

Chapter 19

"When do we leave for court?" Tony asked. Kiki had been giving him her schedule every day, much to Margo's annoyance, and he'd announced first thing that morning he'd be going with her down to the courtroom.

"I leave in a few minutes. You're staying here. Sam didn't mean for you to follow me every place. He just said you're here as security." She slammed her laptop closed, shoved it into her messenger bag and crammed papers in on top.

"What the hell did you think he meant? I'm going with you."

She slung the messenger bag over her shoulder. "You're supposed to protect me, not order me around."

"Protecting you means you do what I say."

"Oh yeah?" She was tired of being followed, babied, protected. Particularly by *him*. "Suppose I don't want to do what you say?"

He stood directly in front of her, his hands balled into fists, which he kept clenching while he talked. "Jesus, Keyes, you're so predictable. You'd argue about anything, wouldn't you, just for the sport of it. Don't you get it? This isn't a sport. If you don't care about your own safety, I do. My ass is on the line here if something happens to you."

The steam went out of her anger as she tried to control the twitch at the corner of her mouth.

"You find that amusing, do you?"

"I just had a sudden image of your local fan club members with pitchforks and torches coming after me if I was responsible for anything happening to your a . . . to you." She turned for the door. "I'm going to the ladies' room. Want to come in with me? I think your groupies meet there to talk about you. Maybe they'll help you get me under control."

He muttered something about driving the Dalai Lama to violence and let her walk in front of him out of her office.

Tony took a seat toward the back of the sparsely populated courtroom. Sitting on the defense side were three people who, from the way they talked to the defendant, knew him. There was a fifty-ish man and woman, the defendant's parents, she assumed.

Paul Dreier, the third person, was in close conversation with the father, who looked familiar, although she didn't know why. She wasn't sure why Paul was there. He was no criminal lawyer. But it did go a long way toward explaining some of his recent comments and suggestions as well as his interest in the case when he was in her office recently.

Gene Orlov, the young man on trial, sat slumped in his chair, pulling at the necktie he was wearing and listening to his lawyer talk to his parents. He'd been very cocky when she'd met with him and his lawyer early on, insisting on going to trial for the armed robbery of a credit union rather than taking a plea bargain. He swore he was innocent. It was a coincidence that the woman who was beaten was a teller who had repeatedly refused to go out with him and had filed a restraining order against him. A coincidence that he had a gun just like the one used in the holdup. And his car, which had been seen leaving the scene, had been stolen from him the morning of the robbery.

But recently the police had turned up a witness. A woman at the ATM outside the credit union had seen the face of the robber before he'd pulled down his ski mask and had immediately picked him out of a photo lineup. She'd been out of the country for two months and had only just realized what she'd seen.

The defendant was considerably less cocky this morning.

The proceedings started on time, the judge being one of Margo's favorites for exactly that reason. After Margo got the police testimony and the circumstantial evidence on the record, she was ready to call the eyewitness to the stand when the judge recessed for lunch.

As she was gathering up her papers and getting ready to leave, the defense attorney came over to the prosecutor's table and asked to talk to Margo in private. He had walked to the brink but had finally decided to deal. *We're done here*, she thought, with some satisfaction.

On the way out of the courtroom, she ran into Dreier. "Paul, what are you doing here? This is out of your bailiwick, isn't it?"

"The kid is. His father isn't. I gather the kid's attorney is willing to deal. Are you going for a stiff sentence?"

"I'm about to see what his attorney's asking for. You got something you want to add to the discussion?"

"Just that his father is a prominent man in the community and would be willing to take on some responsibility for his son if you'll go easy on him. And he'd be in your debt if you would do that. He's the kind of person you would rather have working for you than against you, particularly given what you're involved in."

"Not sure what that means. But thanks for the advice."

"It's more than advice, Margo. It's a strong suggestion. You might be in over your head, here. Be careful."

"Paul, I have to get to my meeting with the defense counsel. I appreciate your interest but I think I can handle this on my own."

She watched Dreier go down the hall toward the older man, the father, who was waiting at the end of the hall. He'd apparently been staring at her the whole time she talked with Dreier. Even at a distance, the way he was looking at her made her uncomfortable. She was glad to get away from his stare and into the conference with his son's attorney.

By the time she had worked out the deal with the defense attorney and his client had accepted, it was late afternoon. Tony was waiting outside the door of the room where she'd been meeting with the defense attorney.

She strode past him, ran the steps to her floor and went into her office with him following close behind. Dropping her bag on the desk with a thump, she said, "I suppose you think I should be grateful you let me negotiate with defense counsel without you sitting there."

"You got out of the courtroom before I could get to you, or I would have been. At least I knew where you were and who was with you."

"Oh, for God's sake, surely you have something better to do than babysit me."

"There're a hell of a lot of other things I could be doing, some of them even more challenging, all of them more interesting, but keeping you alive and breathing is at the top of the 'to do' list I've been given. I don't like this gig any more than you do, sweetheart. But I'm stuck with it. So are you." He went to the door. "We have a meeting at Central Precinct in an hour. Danny'll walk you back to the hotel after that."

She sighed and ran her fingers through her hair. "Yes, Tony. Anything you say, Tony."

"Damn right, anything I say. Glad to see you're finally getting the message."

*

The full team was at the meeting—Jeff, the Portland Police Bureau contingent, the FBI, the two other cops from Long Beach and Seattle. But increasing the number of people involved in the conversation hadn't gotten them anywhere. They reviewed the results from the two crime labs taking Jameson's and Nixon's briefcases apart. Nothing. The Redmond, Washington police had gone back to Nixon's home and searched it again. They'd done the same at Jameson's house. Experts had searched the computers of both victims twice. Nil. Nada. Bupkis.

Sam had scrubbed his hand over his face in frustration so many times while the information was being presented, Margo was sure he had abraded the surface layer of his skin.

Jeff Wyatt, who was running the meeting, said, "We have exactly forty-eight hours to come up with what he wants or we're sending Margo to Beaverton with nothing. And we can't cancel. That runs the risk he hunts her down. Either way . . . " He didn't finish the sentence but everyone in the room knew what he meant.

Danny said, "How did Viktor know that what he wanted wasn't on the flash drive?"

"Yeah, I keep coming back to that, too, Danny," Sam said. "He only saw it. He didn't have to pull it up on a computer. So how did he know it wasn't what he had bought?"

"Have we run the information on those two programs by our Microsoft contact?" Tony asked.

"What's that have to do with it?" Wyatt asked.

"Have we?" Tony persisted.

"I told them what was on the flash drive and they confirmed that both Jameson and Nixon had access to the programs and the information's worth a bundle," Danny answered.

"No, I mean, have we downloaded and emailed what's on that flash drive to them?" Tony asked.

Sam frowned. "What would that accomplish?"

"I'm no computer genius, but I'm wondering if a flash drive with that capacity could really hold all the programming it would take to create a new body-sensitive game and a new version of Microsoft Office with all the bells and whistles."

"But we know that's what's on that flash drive," one of the FBI agents said.

"No, we know there are two files on there with those labels," Tony said, "and we've looked at some of it. But do we know it's the whole program?"

"What are you suggesting?" Jeff Wyatt asked.

"The Genentec scientist in Long Beach—he said something about Viktor demanding a sample of what was for sale before he'd agree to a price. Could that be what Jameson had on the flash drive?"

"Christ," Sam said. "That would explain it. Viktor had already seen the sample. He was expecting the rest of it. Danny, call that guy at Microsoft. Tell him Tony's theory. See what he says."

Twenty minutes later, Danny returned. "Tony was right. I sent him what we have and he says it's just a portion of the program. We're looking for something more like a couple high capacity external hard drives."

"There was nothing like that in either briefcase," Tony said.

"And nothing like that when they searched Nixon and Jameson's houses. We specifically asked them to look for discs and drives," Sam said.

"That leaves . . . what?" Margo asked. "Where else would they stash it? What would they consider a safe place?"

"A safe place. That's it." Sam said, "Keys."

"What's it, Sam?" Margo asked. "What did I say?"

"Not Margo Keyes. The ring of keys in Nixon's bag. Wasn't there a small key? One that could be for a safe deposit box? Danny, would you . . . ?" But his partner had already disappeared to retrieve the ring of keys.

A few phone calls and they'd found the bank where Jameson had rented a safe deposit box a month earlier. After the Redmond police got a court order, the box was opened. Two high capacity hard drives were inside.

They had Viktor's "merchandise."

*

On Thursday, shadowed by her bodyguard, Margo made the trek across the park to Central Precinct for a final run-through before her rendezvous with Viktor. She was dreading it. She had racked her brain trying to find a way to make her back-channel negotiations with Viktor sound like anything other than what they were—a secret she'd kept from Sam and the team. She'd been unable to come up with anything that sounded reasonable, even to her.

Now she was out of time. She had to tell them. It was only one change but it would make Sam angry. And God knows what Tony would say when he found out.

She was relieved to see that the meeting was only the operational team—Danny, Sam and Tony. At least if she was going to have her head ripped off, it wouldn't be in front of the feds. As soon as they all sat down, she took a deep breath and jumped in. "Sam, I'm going to make a slight revision to the plan."

"We're past the point of making changes, Margo," Sam said.

"Not much choice, I'm afraid. I made a deal with Viktor . . . "

Sam's eyes narrowed and he spit words at her like bullets. "What the fuck? What deal?"

"When I told him I needed more time he threatened me, told me I was playing a dangerous game . . . "

Sam brushed her words away with an impatient gesture. "I know that. Get to what I don't know."

"He kept pushing about why I hadn't brought the real merchandise to Blue Lake. Why I wasn't living at home. Why someone was suddenly with me all the time. I said I didn't bring the hard drives with me because I'd lied to you about them. I wanted the money so I let you think the flash drive was what he wanted. And I told him the police moved me after Blue Lake because my boss insisted." She paused for a few heartbeats. "Then, I gave him Tony."

"You WHAT?" Sam said.

"I told him Tony was a cop. Said he was the one who'd seen the email and made the deal because he didn't want me going to Blue Lake alone. Viktor said he knew that."

"You're saying that to give yourself cover," Sam said.

"No, I swear. His exact words were that he was pleased to see I was finally being honest. He said that made him more confident that he could trust me."

"Bullshit," Tony said. "You're just . . . "

"I thought I was pulling it out of thin air but . . . "

"More like out of your ass . . . " Sam said.

"But," she talked over his comment, "he already knew. So, I have to go in alone tomorrow. I'll wear a wire. You can hear the whole thing and come get me out if you need to. I can guarantee you, though, if Tony's with me, the least that will happen is we lose Viktor. At worst . . . well, let's just say it won't be a good outcome for me and maybe not for Tony, either."

"Christ, Margo, this is really fucked up," Sam said.

"Wait just one damn minute. When Tony negotiated with him without talking to you, he was doing a great job. I negotiate with him and I'm a fuck-up?"

"Let's start with the fact that Tony told me about it as soon as it happened. And he's a cop. He knows what he's doing."

"So, am I to understand that you'd trust a cop you'd just met over someone you've worked with for years? Is it because he's a cop or is it because he's a man and I'm neither?" She snapped her fingers. "Damn. Of course, it must be because I don't know how to negotiate. I never do it. Oh, wait, every now and then I do negotiate about minor stuff. You know, the death penalty or life in prison. But I guess that doesn't count as much as emailing a mobster about an imaginary deal. In your world."

"Jesus, Margo, you are . . . " Tony started.

"For Christ's sake, you can't think . . . " Sam said, his voice getting louder with every word.

"Hold it, you three," Danny stood up and held out her hands, like a school crossing guard stopping traffic. "Do I have to send you to neutral corners?"

Sam muttered something that sounded like an apology.

Tony glared at her. Margo refused to look at either of them.

"Now," Danny said as she sat down, "let's get back to tomorrow. Margo, you did good getting him to accept that you've still gone to the dark side."

"You shouldn't have kept it from us," Sam said.

Danny continued to talk only to Margo. "Given the reactions we just saw, I understand why you hesitated to tell these two. Although you did cut it a bit close. Luckily, it doesn't change the plan that much. We'll have you wired, you'll have your cell phone on so we can trace that and the package with the hard drives will have a GPS on it. Once you're out, we take him down." She leaned across the table toward Margo. "Are you sure Viktor bought what you told him?"

Throwing Danny a grateful look, Margo said, "As sure as I can be. It was all done through email so I couldn't read his face but he backed off the threats after I gave him the explanation. Even said at one point my father would have been proud of me."

Margo sat back in her chair and kept her mouth shut for the rest of the discussion as the three detectives went over what they'd be doing now that Tony was with them and not with Margo. She didn't look at him, knowing more would come when they got back to her office.

It didn't take long. The door to her office had barely clicked shut when he lit into her.

"Jesus, Mary and Joseph, have you lost your fucking mind, Keyes? You cannot go waltzing into that grocery store alone for a little chat with a killer."

She walked to her desk and sat down. "Who do you think I chat with on a regular basis, Tony, the Ladies' Altar Guild? And can we keep our voices down? We've provided enough entertainment for my office this week."

"Don't change the subject." But he lowered his voice. "The perps you talk to may be bad guys but they're bad guys who got caught, cleaned up and have a lawyer." He paced back and forth in front of her desk. "What in God's name made you think I'd agree to let you do this?"

"I don't remember giving you the authority to *let* me do anything. It's my life. I make the decisions about it."

Tony stopped and faced her across her desk. "What's this really about, Margo? Has playing with the big boys gone to your head?"

His words felt like a slap across the face. "Playing with the big boys? What the fuck? Who do you think you are to talk to me that way? That's the most arrogant, outrageous . . . "

He held up his hands and took a step back as if to fend off her anger. "Sorry. I'm sorry. That was a bad choice of words."

"That's what you think it is? A bad choice of words? That doesn't come close to describing what . . . "

"I apologize. I shouldn't have said it. I was wrong. But Jesus, I feel like I'm up against the wall here. I'm trying to find a way to keep you safe, but you keep going in the other direction."

"I did fine at Blue Lake and I'll do fine tomorrow."

"You did fine at Blue Lake with me backing you up. Armed. This is different. You don't get paid to do shit like this. You get paid to go into a nice safe courtroom and follow all the rules. This is cop stuff—nothing's routine, everything's unexpected and it's damn dangerous. If I have to, I'll go over Sam's head to make sure you stick to what you're paid to do."

"You're a real pain in the ass, Alessandro."

"Been told that by tougher people than you, Keyes."

Unable to sit still any longer, she jumped up and leaned toward him on tightly balled fists.

"So, your plan is, what? Tattle and get me sidelined? Then what, Ace? Got a next move? No? Well if you can't put up, shut up. I'm tired of playing Nancy Drew with the Hardy Boys in Central Precinct while my colleagues cover for me here. And I'm really tired of having you as a shadow and Danny as a roommate. This will get it taken care of."

"Because you forced the issue so you could run it the way you wanted to."

"That isn't true. He knew you were a cop. What I told him wasn't news. He knows the entire cast of characters—me, you, Danny, Sam, Jeff, the feds. We use me or let him go on his merry way stealing ideas and killing people who get in the way."

"We'll find another way. It's what we get paid to do."

She stared at the ceiling, took a deep breath and then looked at him. "Okay, if that doesn't persuade you, then how about this: he thinks I have those hard drives. If I bail on him tomorrow, how long do you think it'll take for him to come after me? I need to deliver his merchandise and get this target off my back."

He stood with his eyes closed and his lips thinned to a stern, almost invisible, line.

"Tony, please listen to me." Her voice was softer, almost pleading. "This isn't about thrills or wanting to do what you do or forcing everyone to do it my way. It's about getting this guy into custody, using the advantage I have. For the first time, being Kenny Keyes' daughter isn't an embarrassment. I don't expect you to completely understand it, but I do expect you to believe I'm doing this for the right reason. Don't you know me well enough to know that?"

He sighed. "Yes, I do. And I even understand what you're saying, at least a little. But Jesus, Margo, I also know what could happen and it scares the living daylights out of me."

"I'd be lying—and stupid—if I said I wasn't a little scared, too, but you and Sam and Danny and every other law enforcement agency in the region—hell, in the nation—have my back. I'm meeting him in broad daylight in a fairly public place. He trusts me because he thinks I'm as twisted as he is, which gives me a level of safety you wouldn't have." She felt like she was begging by the time she got to the end of her speech. "He's just wants those damn hard drives, Tony. I can deliver hard drives."

"You know what the worst part is? The worst part, the part that really pisses me off, is that I have a feeling you're right—this is the only way left to accomplish what we want and I hate it." He was running his fingers through his hair so hard Margo was afraid he'd pull it all out.

"Tony, I know . . . I wish . . . " She cleared her throat and started again. "I don't want to let what's between us personally get in the way of doing this and I don't think you do either . . . so . . . "

"I can't pretend you're just another person I work with, Margo. Don't ask me to do that."

She suddenly realized that his anger wasn't because she had hidden what she'd done. It was because he was terrified she'd get hurt. No matter what had happened between them, he still cared.

"No, no, I didn't mean that. I meant . . . oh, God, why can't I find the right words?" She looked him in the eye. "Okay, let's try this: I know you've been angry at me. For reasons that . . . well, for reasons that I deserve. But can we call a truce or something? Work out the other stuff when this is over and just get this done?" She walked to his side of the desk and put out her hand to him, as if to shake it. "I'd like to go into tomorrow knowing you're not furious at me and maybe even accept that I know what I'm doing."

He looked at her outstretched hand and, saying nothing, left her office, banging the door closed behind him as he went out.

Margo swallowed hard and sniffed back tears. She'd held out an olive branch and he'd rejected it. That said it all. Still sniffing, she sat at her desk and forwarded the series of emails between herself and Viktor to Sam. As she was sending the last one, there was a knock at the door.

"Come." She didn't look up, assuming it was Kiki wanting to dig into what was going on or Jeff with more advice about the next day.

"A truce sounds good." Tony held out his hand. "Sorry I stormed out of here." She stood up and put out her hand. He covered it with both of his. "I don't know if I can say I accept what you're doing," he continued, "but you absolutely have the right to make the judgment call yourself. Just promise me one thing: you'll give him the hard drives and get the hell out of there. No messing around trying to gather evidence or make a good case or get a confession from him. Let us take care of that."

"I promise. No heroics."

"Right. No heroics. Other than what you're already doing."

She extracted her hand from his and sat down, afraid if she continued touching him she'd give in to the impulse to walk into his arms and nestle her head on his chest. "Listen, I'm not much good around here today. How about I call Danny and see if she's ready to go to the hotel? Maybe you could join us for an early dinner." Although she said it casually, she held her breath waiting for the answer.

"I'd like to, but Sam and Amanda invited me for dinner tonight."

"Oh, well, maybe another time."

"Doubt there'll be too many other times, Margo. Once this is settled, I'll be headed back to Philly." His smile didn't reach his eyes and had no amusement in it. "By this time tomorrow, you'll be free of Danny and me just like you want."

Right, she thought. *Free of you. Just like I want.*

Chapter 20

Pulling into the parking lot of a strip mall just off the Sunset Highway west of Portland, all Margo saw was a *pho* restaurant, a dry cleaners and a payday loan company. Then she spotted a store with signs in Cyrillic and English, vacant stores on either side of it. Assuming that to be her destination, she parked her Forester beside the Lexus and the Cadillac SUV already there.

The homey smell of fresh bread greeted her, as did an older woman behind the counter who motioned her toward a closed door at the back of the store. When she knocked, a male voice with a Russian accent told her to come in. She opened the door to a small, dimly lit room with a desk in the center, the top clear of anything except a computer monitor, a keyboard and a handgun. Sitting at the desk, hands in his lap, was a fiftyish man with graying hair, who looked familiar and not just because he vaguely resembled Nikita Khrushchev.

"Well, I'm here," she said, trying to sound irritated and belligerent. "Let's get this taken care of so I can get on with my plans."

"Miss Keyes, sit down and be quiet."

Margo stood in front of the desk for a moment, trying to look like she was making up her mind whether to go or stay, before she turned her back on Viktor, walked to the chair furthest away from the desk and picked it up. When she returned to where he was waiting, she stared at him again before sitting down.

"I don't know what the hell kind of game you're playing— putting me off, then not listening when I told you I had to outwait the cops, demanding I come out here in two days. I don't like it . . . not one . . . "

His dark eyes bored into hers, unsettling her. His face looked cold, unmoving, and . . . familiar. He had stared at her like that before. When? She'd seen his face briefly at Blue Lake but it had been in shadow, not clear enough to be so familiar.

Then it hit her. Not at Blue Lake. Outside a courtroom. "Jesus, you're Gene Orlov's father, aren't you?"

He nodded. He was playing with the gun. "When you refused to listen to good counsel about my son and about getting involved in this. Didn't you learn anything from your father?"

Margo leaned her forearms on the desk, as if taking him into her confidence, but really to bury her shaking hands under her arms. "What I learned from my father was to take advantage of what falls into your lap. But I'm not making a career out of this, like he did. That's why I've been trying to get the best deal I can."

"I know what you're doing, Miss Keyes. But you don't seem to appreciate what a dangerous game you've been playing."

She sat back in her chair, her shakes under better control. "I know that Jameson and Nixon are dead because they tried to play you off against your former friend Dmitri Petrakov. Who is, I believe, also no longer with us."

Orlov's wolfish grin made her feel like she was Little Red Riding Hood about to become lunch. "No, unfortunately, he is not."

"So, saying I don't know how dangerous you can be is not true. I respect your ability to solve your problems even if I don't approve of your methods."

"Good. We understand each other." He leaned forward and put out his hand. "Now, my merchandise, please."

"Wait. I said I understand you. Now you understand me. I know how much you can get from what's on these hard drives. I want a bigger cut. One hundred thousand isn't enough. I want half a million."

"That's out of . . . "

He was distracted by a sound from the grocery store. Orlov

went to the door, holding the weapon in his hand, listened for a moment, opened the door slightly and said something in Russian. The old woman responded in kind.

Then a man's voice interrupted. It sounded like English but was quiet enough that Margo couldn't make out anything except the rude, impatient tone. Orlov answered in English, "I will take care of it my way," before returning to the desk. "Half a million is too much. But I might be willing to go to one-hundred thousand for each of the two hard drives."

She sat back in the chair and crossed her legs, tilted the chair back slightly and ran her hand through her hair. "Two-hundred and fifty thousand for both and they're yours," she said.

"You can be your father's daughter, can't you? At least you learned how to negotiate in ways that would make him proud."

She shrugged it off. "So, do we have a deal?"

"Yes. I have $100,000 here for you." He pulled a briefcase from under the desk and dropped it in front of her. "You give me my merchandise and I will put the rest of the money in your bank account."

"For that you get one and only because I'm a nice person. I'll take the other hard drive to my bank and put it in my safe deposit box. When can you have the rest of the money?"

He stared long and hard at her. "Tomorrow."

"I'll meet you at my bank tomorrow at noon. And when I see that the money's in my account, you'll get the second one."

"Tomorrow at noon at your bank." He passed the briefcase full of money to her.

Margo took a padded envelope from her shoulder bag and wrote the address of her bank on the outside. "Here's where I bank. And here," she removed one hard drive and put it back in her bag then slid the envelope across the desk to him, "is what you just bought."

He picked up the envelope and looked inside. She used the

distraction to grab the briefcase and walk toward the door to the grocery store. When she felt his arm around her neck and his gun in her back, she realized he hadn't been distracted at all.

"I thought we had a deal." She coughed and moved her head, trying to release the pressure on her windpipe.

"Did you really believe you could just walk out of here without giving me what I want?" He released his hold on her throat to reach for the strap of her shoulder bag. As he did, his hand brushed against her chest. He came around to face her and ripped open her blouse, exposing the wire she was wearing.

"Where are the police who are listening to us?"

"The last time I saw them, they were at police headquarters," she said, her voice less steady than she would have liked.

He said in a very loud voice, "She is wired."

The door to the grocery store opened.

"Margo, I thought you were smarter than this," Paul Dreier said as he entered.

Chapter 21

Dreier ripped the wire from Margo's chest. She yelled, "Jesus, Paul . . . " before Orlov muffled her mouth with his arm.

When he'd destroyed the listening device, he rummaged in her purse for her cell phone, which met the same fate. Then he said to his partner, "We don't have much time. They know something's gone wrong and will be here in minutes. Take the hard drives to the airport. Our contact will meet you there. I'll take care of her."

He raised the weapon he was carrying.

*

Margo woke in a dark and dusty place to the sound of a smoothly purring engine and the feeling of something hard pressed against her stomach. From the pain in the back of her head, she didn't have to guess what Paul had done with the raised weapon. After that, he'd apparently bound her hands and feet with something and gagged her.

A little late, she realized she should have recognized the Lexus parked out front of the grocery store as Paul's. Apparently she was riding in it, lying face down in the foot well of the back seat and covered with some kind of itchy, dusty blanket.

When she tried to move, the hump in the center of the car prevented her from shifting her body. Unless whoever had been listening figured it out, she was on the way to some place she was sure she didn't want to go.

The sound of sirens wailing behind them gave her hope that someone had figured it out. But Paul sped up and Margo's elation passed as they cut from one lane to another and the sirens faded. As her head bounced from side to side with the swaying car, she figured Paul might be saved the trouble of killing her. The consequences of the high-speed chase would take care of it quite nicely.

Her hopes and the sirens rose and fell for what seemed like an eternity. Then suddenly she was thrown violently against the backseat as Paul swerved to the right and made a dizzying turn around a sharp curve. Cars screeched to a stop. There were explosive sounds. The Lexus came to an abrupt halt. Two other cars banged into them. There was an unfamiliar sound inside the car. Then silence.

In a few moments, there was a cacophony of voices. "Police! Put your hands where we can see them." "What the hell is going on here?" "Move. This is a crime scene." "My car's wrecked." "Open the door."

And the most welcome, a familiar voice saying, "Where's Margo?"

The back door opened and the blanket was pulled away. "Jesus, sugar," Tony said as he extricated her from the foot well. He carried her to a nearby patrol car and sat on the passenger side, holding her so hard and so close she had trouble breathing. After a few seconds, he loosened his grip and began to unbind her wrists and ankles.

When she was freed, he sat with her on his lap, holding her tightly while Sam negotiated who would be doing what and with whom among the law enforcement agencies of the state, two cities, two counties and the federal government. The security of his embrace, the smell of his cologne, the strength of his arms were exactly what she needed. She didn't fight him.

When it was all sorted out Tony drove her back into Portland. Their thirty-minute ride back to Central Precinct started out silently. She sat with her eyes shut aware of his nearness, wanting to touch him, but afraid he'd push her away. When she opened her eyes, she saw he was glancing over at her.

"That must have been a helluva ride."

"It wasn't fun. How'd you know to follow Paul's car?"

"You're not going to like the answer but . . . I asked Sam to put a GPS in your shoulder bag while Danny was wiring you up."

"Shit. You really did bug me this time, didn't you, Alessandro?"

"Yup. With the tracer on the hard drives going one way and no cell phone signal, we'd have been chasing the wrong thing if it hadn't been for the one in your bag."

"Okay, I'm grateful. But how'd you know to stop Paul's Lexus?"

"Danny. She thought she recognized his voice. Then, when you called him Paul, she was sure. She pulled up the information on his car just as we heard that a county mountie was on his tail for reckless driving. When that came over the radio, we knew exactly what to look for. Got the state police to close the freeway and herd him to a spike strip and that's that."

"He didn't put up much fight."

"Airbags can knock you silly if they hit you right."

"Airbag. That's the sound I heard."

At the Justice Center, Tony hovered a bit, bringing her coffee and a sandwich, some solvent to get the remains of the tape adhesive off her wrists and ankles. Margo wasn't sure if the tears she felt close to the surface were because of her car ride or his attention.

Once Sam returned, everyone involved spent the rest of the day beginning to put the pieces together. They started with three Russians: in Portland, Vasily Orlov, aka Viktor. The dead Russian in Newark, a former colleague of Orlov's and the erstwhile competitor for control of the industrial espionage operation, Dmitri Petrakov. The third Russian, who made it out of Portland International Airport on a plane bound for Frankfurt, Germany just ahead of the police sent to arrest him, was Yuri Volkov. They had alerted the authorities in Frankfurt to pick him up when the plane landed.

All three of them had known each other in Russia before coming to the U.S., involved in shady deals but clever enough to avoid arrest. Somehow, Orlov had found Paul Dreier and, because of Dreier's contacts with businesses not likely to ask questions about how their attorney had access to information that would help their bottom line, they formed an alliance. It was a nasty, if lucrative, business that had resulted in a half-dozen deaths and millions of dollars of damage to businesses more honest than Dreier's clients.

*

By the time Margo had gotten most of what she knew on the record, it was getting dark. She was beginning to have trouble concentrating. When she asked Sam for the third time when he wanted her to come to Central Precinct the following day, he said, "You're fried, Margo. Let's finish this tomorrow. Tony, why don't you drive her home?"

Margo pushed herself back from the table and stood up, a little shaky but happy at the prospect of going home. All she needed was something to eat and a good night's sleep. "I can drive myself, Sam."

"You've lost your stuffing and I don't want to get called out to an accident scene where I get to watch them pry your body out of a car that's wrapped around a bridge abutment."

"I can take care of myself. I'm not some . . . "

Danny interrupted. "Margo, remember the waiting room at Emanuel?"

Margo remembered. "Okay, Tony can drive me home."

She was almost out the door when Sam said, "Counselor? Nice work today."

Afraid if she said anything her voice would crack, she nodded acknowledgement of the compliment.

As he merged onto the freeway toward Margo's home, Tony said. "Sam's right. You were terrific." He hesitated for a moment before adding, "I was proud of you."

She gulped down a lump in her throat. "Thanks, that means a lot."

After a few minutes of embarrassed silence he said, "Can I ask? What did Danny mean about the waiting room?"

"It's kind of a long story but, short version, about a year ago, Sam got shot by a guy who'd killed two people and been stalking Amanda. Amanda, Danny and I spent a long time in the hospital waiting room while they put Sam back together. Amanda was like a balloon with the air let out. We wouldn't let her drive home by herself."

"Jesus, no wonder you're all friends. That's a hell of an experience to go through together."

"Yeah, I'm not likely to forget it."

"Was he was shot in the left shoulder?"

"How'd you know?"

"He rubs his left shoulder, moves it sometimes, like it bothers him. I wondered if he'd been injured." He shook his head. "I've seen marriages break up when something like that happens to a cop. Amanda must be pretty strong to have her husband . . . "

"They weren't married when it happened. Got married not too long after."

"Now I admire her even more."

"Sam says if they could cut through the brush and find their way to the altar, anyone can."

"Do you think he's right?"

Luckily, they were at her parking lot and she didn't have to respond. She started to get her key card out of her shoulder bag so he could open the gate but Tony pulled the extra one she had given him from the side pocket in the door. After he used it, he dropped it back into the door pocket. She knew she should ask him to return it to her but couldn't bring herself to do it.

He parked and she opened the door. "Thanks for the ride. I appreciate it."

"Wait. I'm walking you to the door. Don't want you to collapse on the dock for Mr. Todd to find."

At her front door, she fumbled with the key, eventually getting it in the lock. But she didn't turn it; she was hyperventilating.

"Margo? What's wrong?"

"It's silly but I have this feeling there's something bad on the other side of the door."

He removed her hand from the key and unlocked the door. "Want some company for a while?"

"Would you mind?" He shook his head and she was relieved he understood.

Once into the house, she dropped her purse on a chair and stared at her living room as if seeing it for the first time.

"How about I take a look around," he said and started down the hall toward the guest room.

"Thanks. I know it's weird but . . . " She went into the kitchen. "Want a cup of coffee or something? I'm going to make myself some cocoa. Maybe something warm will help." From the refrigerator she brought out a carton of milk.

"Hot chocolate sounds good." He was at the foot of the steps, about to go upstairs, when he saw her on tiptoe reaching for the cocoa. "I'll get that for you."

She brought down the container. "No thanks, I've got it." Her hand began to shake. She grasped it with her other hand, which only made it worse because it, too, was shaking. The lid popped off and cocoa powder scattered over the counter.

Tony closed the distance between them in a few steps and took the can from her. One look at her face and he wrapped his arms around her. "It's okay. It's over."

She began to sniffle. "I'm going to cry, aren't I?"

"Yeah, you are."

When she'd finished pouring a significant amount of the fluid in her body out through her eyes and onto his shirt, she fumbled for a paper towel. He got there first, pulled one off, gently wiped her face and held it so she could blow her nose.

"You must think I'm some kind of wuss." She could feel her eyes puffing up and her nose beginning to run again.

"I think you're a smart and resourceful woman who's had a really bad day at work. You're doing great."

Still sniffing, she reached for another paper towel. "This is embarrassing. Cops don't cry."

"Sometimes they do. And the ones who don't can do really stupid things instead."

"Oh, God, I've made a mess of your shirt." She pointed to the wet spots streaked with mascara and make-up now decorating his chest.

He glanced down and shrugged his shoulders. "This one was headed for the laundry anyway." Taking the towel from her hand, he dabbed at her eyes. "How 'bout I make the hot chocolate. Go upstairs and get into bed. I'll bring it up when it's ready."

Chapter 22

When did it get to be so bright? Were all the lights in the marina on? Margo sat up, looked out at the river and realized the light wasn't courtesy of the power company. It was morning. She barely remembered coming up the stairs, let alone falling into bed. But she obviously had.

From downstairs, she heard the sounds of Charlie Byrd's guitar jazz and a man talking. Then she smelled coffee. What the hell? She was groggy but she was awake. Who was down there? Maybe someone broke in. Another Russian had found her. But what kind of intruder would make coffee and play music?

She'd better go find out what was going on. Throwing her legs out from under the sheet, she banged into her bedside table. There was a cup of something on the nightstand. It looked like chocolate milk. Right, she'd been making cocoa when she got home. Before she could connect the dots, she saw her reflection in the mirror. Why had she put on a man's pajama top with her bikini panties?

She'd sort that out later. Now, she needed her cell phone and something she could use as a weapon, just in case. Looking around her room, she couldn't see her phone. And there were few weapons options. The only choices seemed to be an original Amanda St. Claire glass art piece or a ten-pound hand weight. The art glass was heavier and more dangerous to use as a weapon but it was also much more valuable. The hand weight, it was.

Four steps down the staircase, and the dots began to connect. *Tony.* He'd been with her last night. Had volunteered to make cocoa. And that was his voice. He was on the phone, telling someone she was asleep, but would be at Central Precinct that afternoon.

Just as he was about to finish the conversation, he looked up the steps. "Sleeping Beauty has awakened. Want to talk to her?" He handed his cell phone to her. "It's Jeff."

"Morning, Jeff. Sorry I'm not . . . "

"You don't have to explain anything. Both Tony and Sam called and told me everything. And Sam said—I'm quoting here—you were great yesterday. High praise from him."

"I must still be dreaming if he was that complimentary. I heard Tony tell you I have another meeting over there this afternoon. I'll come see you after that."

"The only reason to drop in today is so I can congratulate you. That and maybe you can help get the reporters who've been hanging around cleared out."

"Reporters. *Damn.* I better call Fiona. I promised her first shot at what I knew because she put off running her big story."

"Take care of Fiona and get squared away with Sam. And get some rest. Tony says you were pretty beat after your adventures."

She ended the conversation and handed the phone back to Tony.

"What were you planning to do with that?" he asked, indicating the hand weight, a slight smile on his face. "It wasn't meant for me, was it?"

She put the weight on the counter and ignored his question. "Were you here all night?"

"No, Margo, I went to the hotel and changed into another shirt that looks like this," he said indicating the make-up-smeared—and now wrinkled—shirt he was wearing. Apparently the look on her face forced a change of direction in the conversation. "Not ready for humor yet, I see. Yes, I stayed. When I brought you the hot chocolate, you'd fallen asleep but you were restless. I rubbed your back for a while and you settled down. When I started to move away from you, you didn't seem to want me to go."

"Where did you sleep?"

"Next to you. But I was a gentleman. Your wardrobe made that easier than I might have expected." He fussed with the coffee pot. "Want some coffee? I just made it."

"I guess I should thank you." She could feel tears beginning again and swallowed, hardening the tone of her voice to keep from showing her emotion.

"You wanted someone here. I stayed." He brought two mugs down from the shelf and poured coffee into them. "Sorry it's black. I used the last of the milk to make your hot chocolate." He handed one to her.

She put it down on the counter. "I don't understand why you stayed. I didn't ask you to."

"Jesus, is cross-examination of my motives what you call a truce? I thought after yesterday maybe . . . " He banged the mug he was holding down on the counter. "I obviously misunderstood. I apologize. I'll leave and get out of your way." He wiped off the coffee that had splashed out of the mug onto his fingers, grabbed his jacket from the back of a dining room chair and strode toward the door.

Before he could get there, she put out her hand. "Tony, please. I didn't mean to sound like I didn't want you here . . . don't want you here. I just can't figure out why you stayed when I've been so . . . so inhospitable."

He stopped. Without turning around, he said, "Why do you have to take everything apart and try to reassemble it so it fits your idea of how it should be?"

Her hand slowly sagged to her side and she sniffled as if she was about to cry again.

He must have heard because he faced her and said in a gentler tone, "I stayed because I thought it would make you feel better. Why's that suspicious?"

"It's not. But I don't deserve it. I've been scared and stupid and stubborn . . . "

His mouth skewed into a wry expression. "Yeah, you have been."

"I seem to say everything wrong when I try to talk to you. Please. Don't go. Give me another chance to say it right."

He came across the room and stood in front of her. "That's not a bad start. Go on."

"Yesterday, all I wanted was to hold on to you when you got me out of that damned car. But I couldn't."

"Well, you were duct-taped." The smile was now approaching normal.

"That's not it. I didn't think you'd want me to. I was afraid you'd push me away." She stopped and looked up at him. "I thought maybe you'd given up on me, on us. I never answered the question you asked before you left; I couldn't figure out how to talk to you when you got back. I thought I'd lost my chance to make it right."

"Do you want to make it right?" He circled her waist with his arms and she sighed as she sank into his embrace.

"God, yes. More than anything." She pulled back and looked into his eyes. "If it's not too late, I'd like to answer the question you asked. Yes, I want us to be together. I can't imagine my life anymore without you. It's just that . . . just that . . . " She shook her head as if the words were stuck and she was trying to get them loose enough to come out.

"Just that what, Margo?" He smoothed the worry lines in her forehead.

"It's just that, I need to know you forgive me. I need you to say you aren't mad at me. I need . . . "

"You need to stop talking so I can kiss you."

"Oh, yes, you need to kiss me." She bracketed his face with her hands, the smile on his face reached his candy-bar eyes and she let herself get lost in them.

His lips were soft and tasted wonderful, like the sweetest dessert, the best wine she'd ever had. She dropped her head back and he released her enough to kiss the pulse in her throat before kissing her forehead, the tip of her nose and each cheek. He ran his thumbs along her cheekbones, and then he kissed her again, slanting the angle of his mouth to capture hers completely, his intensity making her breathless. When he released her, she clung to him as if the house had slipped its moorings and he was the only stability.

"Sugar, there is one thing about last night. I wasn't kidding when I said what you have on made it easier to behave myself. That pajama top . . ."

She glanced at her arm and laughed. "It's another long story."

"I have a lot of time for this one, Margo."

Trying hard to suppress a laugh, she said, "Actually, I'm not sure why I'm wearing it. I don't remember putting it on. I guess I just grabbed the first thing I could find."

"Is this left over from some guy you were . . . ?"

"The only other person who's worn this is Sam."

"Sam Richardson? You slept . . . ?"

"No, Tony, of course I didn't. He wore it when he was in the hospital after he was shot. It came from this guy I was seeing for a while. It was a pretty casual relationship; at least, that's what I thought. Until, out of the blue on Valentine's Day, he gave me a beautifully wrapped box in which I found a fluffy nightgown, which he said he'd keep at his house, and these pajamas, which he said I was to keep at mine. Then, he said, when we decided it was time to sleep together, we'd be prepared, no matter whose house we were at. We didn't see each other much after that."

Margo was sure everyone in the marina heard Tony roar with laughter. When he could finally talk, he said, "Jesus, Margo, how come you aren't still with him organizing each other's lives out into the next millennium?"

"That's a terrible thing to say, Alessandro. I'm not like that." When he didn't respond right away, she asked, "Am I?"

"No, you're not *that* bad. But promise me you won't wear that again when I'm sleeping with you. In fact, maybe we should go upstairs and get you out of it. Don't you need to go back to bed for a while?"

"I'm fine. I'm not sleepy . . . "

"Neither am I."

When they got to her room, he opened the drawer of the bedside table and smiled. "So, you expected me back," he said as he pulled out a foil packet and handed it to her.

"Not expected, hoped." She started to unbutton the pajama top she was wearing.

He stopped her. "Let me." He unbuttoned the top and slipped it down her arms, kissing her shoulders gently as the fabric slid off her body. Then he got on his knees and took off her bikinis, kissing up her thighs to the dark cluster of curls at the top. He kissed her there, tonguing the nub of her clitoris, sucking gently on it. The combination of his tongue, his teeth and his mouth on her made her legs go weak. But before she could climax, he laid her down on the bed.

She was restless with wanting him, her every cell crying out for the touch of him. It was like the first night they'd made love, when she'd watched him undress only now she knew what making love with him was like and she wanted it even more.

And this time, it was in the full light of day. No shadows hid the perfect shoulders, the pecs and abs that made her fingers want to run over the ridges and tickle the valleys between. And when he shed his trousers and boxers in one, her breath hitched, her mouth watered and her arms reached for him, for his arms, his mouth, his penis ready for her.

Joining her in bed, he laid on his side, helped her roll the condom over his erection, and then snugged her hips against his. She rocked against his shaft, her arms tight around his chest. "Make love to me, Tony, please." She was sure he could hear the need in her voice, feel the heat of her body as she curled her leg over his hip.

"Soon, sugar, soon. But first," he caressed her breasts, bringing her nipples to diamond hard points. "This is where I wanted to be last night," he whispered. "And here." He sucked gently at the base of her throat. "And here," as he finally kissed her mouth. His eyes were dark with desire, but his mouth, his hands were gentle, tender. She moaned against his mouth as he deepened the kiss, his tongue lazily exploring hers. Her hands played over his amazing body, finding a home on the hard muscles of his butt, drawing him to her.

Taking his time, he slowly entered her. No mad, passionate dash to climax, his lovemaking was sweet and slow, as if they had all the time in the world. She got lost in the warmth, the affection—the "love" part of lovemaking. He didn't have to touch her clitoris for her to come—the slow and tender rhythm of his body did it for her.

They lay silently curled in one and other's arms, watching the river as they usually did after they made love but this morning her beloved river couldn't hold her attention for very long.

"I didn't finish my apology," she began.

He skimmed his hand along the curve of her hip. "I don't think it was lacking in anything."

"Please, Tony. I need to finish it." She took a deep breath. "The only thing that matters to me is being with you. So whatever it takes, whatever you want, let's do it."

He pulled back from her and frowned. "Whatever I want? How about whatever *we* want? This isn't a decision for one of us to make."

"But I thought . . . didn't you say . . . ?"

"Margo, I asked if we could begin to talk about the future, *we* and *begin* being the operative words. I wasn't asking to pick out our kids' names, although I would like to put in a good word for the name Joseph when we get to that conversation."

She rolled her eyes and laughed.

He went on as if she wasn't laughing. "If you'd said that one thing you said a little while ago—that you can't imagine being without me—I'd have had the answer I was looking for."

"I was an idiot. Can you forgive me?"

"If you'll forgive me."

"For what?"

"How long have I known you? I knew better than to bring up something like that just as I was about to walk out the door for a couple days. My timing sucked. When I walked into the room for that first meeting after I got back, you looked scared to death. No woman who wasn't under arrest has ever looked at me like that."

"I'm not scared any more. I know what I want."

"I do, too. Do you trust us to get it?"

"Yes, of course I trust us—trust you." She drew him close and kissed him. "I can't believe I've wasted all these days when I could have had you here to myself."

"We wouldn't have been here after what happened at Blue Lake. You'd have been in a hotel room with Danny. And it's not a bad thing that I've had a few days on my own. I found out I really like Portland, even when I'm not with you."

"You're just being nice."

"When I have this golden opportunity to guilt you about kicking me out of your bed, do you really think I'd do that, Keyes?"

Chapter 23

The payback for Fiona's help in getting her cover story held was a long phone call during which she squeezed every detail out of Margo she could. By the time they had gone through the whole adventure, Fiona knew everything from the smell of the bread in the Russian grocery store to the sticky feel of adhesive tape holding a wire in place to the metallic taste of fear as a car sped along an interstate to places unknown.

In return, Fiona shared some of the information she'd gotten from her other interviews. How Jameson and Nixon had gotten involved with the two Russian mobsters, they didn't know yet. Somehow they had been in negotiations with both of them, teasing them with bits of information which had been apparently loaded onto not one, but two flash drives while they held onto the entire programs, trying to drive the price up; a tactic that had resulted in their deaths.

Fiona reported that Paul Dreier had retained a big-time criminal lawyer from the East Coast who was asserting that Dreier had been used by the Russians. The only thing Dreier was willing to admit was that he'd hit Margo. He claimed he had been trying to get her out of harm's way because he feared what Vasily Orlov would do to her.

Sam, Fiona said, thought that wrapping her in duct tape and heading for Larch Mountain where dead bodies can be hidden for years was an odd way to get Margo out of harm's way. But then, Sam had added, maybe he wasn't headed for Larch Mountain. Maybe he'd asked Margo to lunch at the Multnomah Falls Lodge and wouldn't take no for an answer.

*

Margo had this foolish idea that she would go into work on Monday and things would be back to normal as if the events of Friday had never happened. But everyone in the courthouse from the security guard to her colleagues had seen at least one version of her adventure on the front-page of the daily paper, online after her interview with Fiona or on one of the multiple local television newscasts.

The Portland Police Bureau, the FBI, and all the other law enforcement agencies involved had their share of coverage, too, but the success of the entire operation was laid at the feet of the "Golden Girl" DA, as one newscast called her.

So on Monday, fifteen minutes after she arrived at her office, the phone started ringing. And it kept on ringing non-stop. Then there were the colleagues who "just dropped in to see how you are" and stayed to ask questions. Not to mention the phone calls from Sam, also asking questions, his inquiries more in the official line.

If her phone calls were time-consuming, her email was overwhelming. People she hadn't heard from in years, having seen the AP story that went out on the wire, sent messages. Even Celeste Alessandro sent a message after she'd seen the piece in the *Inquirer*.

Eventually Margo gave up the idea she'd get back to her caseload, sat back in her chair, drank innumerable lattes supplied by Kiki and answered the same questions over and over. Yes, she'd been scared. No, she didn't think she would leave the DA's office for a career in police work. Yes, she was happy to have played a pivotal role in such an important case. No, she wasn't going to take time off to write a book. And GMA hadn't called for an interview.

After a few hours, things settled down a little and she decided to find a scone or something to sop up all the coffee sloshing around in her stomach. As she headed for the elevator she saw Greer Payne burst out of Jeff's office, obviously crying, after what was apparently a bad meeting.

Margo genuinely felt sorry for her colleague. For the first time, her judgment about men had been bad and probably career limiting.

*

Tuesday afternoon Kiki came into the office, her eyes dreamy, as if she'd just seen her high school crush. Instead, she'd seen Margo's.

"Looks like Tony came to say *arrivederci*," she said. "God, I'm going to miss seeing him around here." Margo winced and Kiki immediately said, "I'm sorry. I didn't think."

"It's okay. It's true and I have to deal with it."

Margo walked out of her office and saw Tony at the door of Jeff's office. Jeff was smiling as they shook hands, then he clapped Tony on the back in one of those pseudo-guy hugs. Tony saw she was watching and came across to her office.

"What're you doing here, *detectivo*?"

"Playing messenger. What're you up to, *avocatessa*?"

"Trying unsuccessfully to get back into my routine. Dinner in town or at my place?"

"Your place. I'll meet you outside the Justice Center at six." He leaned over and for the first time, kissed her in her office.

*

The next day Tony left for Philly. At the airport, they stood outside security with their arms around each other until he couldn't put off going through to his gate any longer. She watched him walk down the concourse until he was out of sight, and then went home to have the cry she'd been suppressing all morning.

The case she was to take to court that Friday ended up with a continuance, irritating her because she had counted on it to distract her. Over the next few weeks she talked to Tony every evening she could, given different time zones and the demands of their jobs, and emailed or texted during the day. But she missed waking up in the morning with him next to her and she looked up, expecting him to appear every time she heard a man's footsteps coming toward her office.

Eventually her caseload picked up and she was able to bury herself in work. Unfortunately, that also meant that a trip to Philly wasn't going to happen any time soon. A month after he left, Margo was cross-checking her schedule with flights to any East Coast city within train distance of Philadelphia when Jeff came into her office to tell her they would be taking the Russians to a grand jury the following week and both she and Tony would be called as witnesses. He'd be in town for as long as the grand jury needed him.

Jeff was about to leave when he said, "Oh, I have something that was delivered here for him. Would you give it to him? I imagine you'll see him before I do." He handed her a business-sized envelope, gave her an enigmatic smile and left.

Margo fingered the envelope. It was thin, probably only one page. She inspected the front. It bore the seal of the city of Portland and was addressed to Detective Anthony S. Alessandro. There was no address. No stamp or postmark. She flipped it over. It was sealed.

She put it down on her desk and picked up the deposition she'd been reading before Jeff had come in. But the envelope drew her attention to it in spite of her best efforts to resist, beckoning to her like new shoes in the window of Nordstrom's, or the smell of coffee in the morning, or brownies baking or . . .

The phone rang, interrupting her thoughts of things that tempted her. She stuffed the envelope in her messenger bag and answered the call. She got so involved in the conversation she forgot about what was buried in her briefcase.

*

On the evening Tony was due to arrive in Portland, Margo was cleaning up the kitchen after dinner when her cell phone rang.

She glanced at the number then eagerly answered. "Hey, you. Are you about to leave Chicago?"

"Not exactly."

"Oh, please don't tell me you missed your connection. I've been looking forward to seeing you all day."

"Maybe we can do something about that. Go to the door, sugar."

"Go to the door? Why?"

"For once, would you do what I ask without an argument? Go open your door."

When she did, she found him standing there with a big grin on his face. She shrieked and jumped into his arms. Finally, they released each other but she kept hold of his arm as he walked into the house.

"You're early."

"My flight into Chicago was way early, and a flight attendant who thought it was sweet I was on my way to see my girlfriend got me on an earlier flight. I had to run like hell from one gate to another but I made it."

He took her in his arms and kissed her again. Had there been someone there to try, a piece of paper couldn't have been slipped anywhere between their bodies.

When they broke from their embrace, she asked if he wanted something to eat or drink. He replied, "Not right now. I hear you have something for me from Jeff."

"Oh, yeah, I forgot about that." She dug the envelope out of her messenger bag and gave it to him. "What is it, do you know?"

"You didn't open it?"

"It's addressed to you. Opening another person's mail is a federal offense."

"That wasn't mailed. And you have my permission to open it."

"Well, then." She tore into the envelope and pulled out the folded paper. It was from the chief of police and simply said it was confirming that Detective Anthony S. Alessandro, currently with the Philadelphia Police Department, would, as of October fifteenth of this year, join the Portland Police Bureau. After a course at the Police Academy and upon passing an exam, he would be at the rank of detective.

"I don't understand. How . . . ? Was it Jeff? Is that why he had this? He did this?"

"Yeah, he did. He's been afraid he'd lose you so he called in some political favors to get me into the Police Bureau ahead of everyone else. He asked me to keep it quiet until he was sure it would work out."

"He never said a word. But you have to retake the detective exam? That doesn't seem fair."

"I'll take any exam they want. I'll go back in uniform if I have to. Jeff got me a slot in the Portland Police Bureau and I'm grateful. I have to play basketball every Saturday during the season on the team Jeff and the chief play for, but . . . "

"I should have known that's how he pulled this particular rabbit out of the hat." She picked up his suitcase. "Oh, there's also a package here from The Fairchild Gallery addressed to you. It's not big enough to contain Liz or I would have punched air holes in it so she . . . "

"You can open that, too, sugar. It's an early birthday present for you."

Inside the carefully packaged container was the piece of Amanda St. Claire's glass that Margo had admired the first night Tony had been in town.

She was sure her eyes were suspiciously shiny and she had a huge lump in her throat that made it hard to speak. "Thank you. You shouldn't have . . . it's so expensive . . . you're wonderful."

"I figured as long as there might be a chance I'd be living here with you, I'd be able to enjoy it, too."

"A *chance* you'll be living here? Of course you'll live here. I mean, if you want to."

"I learned my lesson, Keyes. I'm not taking anything for granted."

"We might have to convince Mr. Todd it's okay. He's been asking me when you're going to make an honest woman of me."

"Maybe we should talk about that before I go back to Philly." He took her hand and headed to the steps. "But right now, I have this urge to watch the river from your bed."

They made it upstairs in seconds. His suitcase didn't get there until the next morning.

About the Author

Peggy Bird lives with her husband in Vancouver, Washington where she writes and does kiln-formed glass across the Columbia River from Portland, Oregon where her three daughters, assorted grandchildren and grand-dogs, and Bullseye Glass live.

If you liked this story, you might enjoy *Beginning Again* or *Loving Again*, both available now from Crimson Romance.

In the mood for more Crimson Romance? Check out *Her New Worst Enemy* by Christy McKellen at CrimsonRomance.com.

CPSIA information can be obtained at www.ICGtesting.com
Printed in the USA
LVOW122359020713

341300LV00012B/223/P